ELTONSBRODY

EDGAR MITTELHOLZER (1909-1965) is often considered to be the first novel-ist from the West Indies to earn an international reputation for his fiction, as well as the first professional novelist to emerge from the English-speaking Caribbean. Beginning with his first book, *Creole Chips*, which he self-published in 1937, Mittelholzer would go on to publish more than twenty volumes of fiction, as well as two volumes of nonfiction, including the auto-biography *A Swarthy Boy* (1963). His best-known works include *A Morning at the Office* (1950), which one critic cited as having begun 'the great decade of the West Indian novel', the *Kaywana* trilogy (1952-58), and the ghost story *My Bones and My Flute* (1955).

Edgar Mittelholzer

ELTONSBRODY

WITH A NEW INTRODUCTION BY
JOHN THIEME

VALANCOURT BOOKS

Eltonsbrody by Edgar Mittelholzer
First published by Secker & Warburg, London, 1960
This edition first published 2017

Published by Valancourt Books, Richmond, Virginia
http://www.valancourtbooks.com

ISBN 978-1-943910-62-5 (trade paperback)
ISBN 978-1-943910-63-2 (hardcover)
Also available as an electronic book.

All Valancourt Books publications are printed on acid free paper that meets all ANSI standards for archival quality paper.

Cover: Reproduction of the original dust jacket art by Renato Fratini

Set in Dante MT

INTRODUCTION

EDGAR MITTELHOLZER was born in New Amsterdam, Guyana (then British Guiana) in 1909 into a mixed-race family of German-Swiss, French, English and African descent. In his autobiography of his early years, *A Swarthy Boy* (1963), he writes about being torn between two opposing impulses, the 'Idyll Element' and the 'Warrior Element', and themes of psychic division run throughout his work. He espoused the Germanic side of his heritage and had a lifelong love of Nietzsche's philosophy and Wagner's music.[1] Apparently untroubled by their association with fascism in the 1930s, he associated these German influences with strength of character, and a struggle between envisioned strong and weak facets of personality is a recurrent theme in his fiction, achieving its fullest expression in his epic *Kaywana* trilogy (1952-58),[2] which spans more than three centuries of Guyanese history.

As the 'swarthy' son of a mixed-race family, Mittelholzer was acutely conscious of being a disappointment to his 'negro-phobe' father and throughout his life his wrestling with what he saw as a dual identity provided the driving force for much of his writing, including Gothic works such as *Eltonsbrody* (1960). Several of his novels, beginning with his first to be published, *Corentyne Thunder* (1941), include characters who contemplate suicide, and suicide becomes an increasingly prominent theme in his later fiction: *The Wounded and the Worried* (1962) brings four would-be suicides together for a house party, and in the final pages of his last work, *The Jilkington Drama* (1965), published in the year of his death, the protagonist kills himself in a manner which foreshadows Mittelholzer's own meticulously planned suicide. Apparently inspired by the ending of Wagner's Götterdamerung,[3] he burnt himself to death in an English field. He had attempted suicide on at least two previous occasions.

In Mittelholzer's earliest fiction, his fascination with troubled mental states is held in check by an attempt to represent observed social realities. *Corentyne Thunder* deals with the East Indian peasantry living on the coast of Guyana's easternmost county, Berbice, where he had spent his early years. *A Morning at the Office* (1950) offers a minutely detailed account of events in a Trinidadian office during the course of a single morning. For Mittelholzer, this novel was 'a grand tract nicely dressed up […] in the guise of a novel',[4] and it displays an obsessive concern with the minutiae of responses to 'race' and colour in the late colonial era. However, realism was not Mittelholzer's forte and with his third novel, *Shadows Move Among Them* (1951), he deserted the naturalistic veneer of the previous two in favour of a Gothic mode that allowed him to explore inner mental states without the constraints of having to make his characters conform to social norms. He had found his métier and *Shadows Move Among Them* paved the way for several subsequent novels, in which the Gothic liberated him to write about the preoccupations that most fascinated him. *My Bones and My Flute* (1955), set in the Guyanese interior, and *Eltonsbrody*, set in Barbados, are among the finest instances of this side of his writing.

Eltonsbrody opens with remarks that indicate a highly self-conscious use of the Gothic genre. The novel's narrator, Woodsley,[5] a commercial artist and landscape painter, says he has no capacity for handling colour on paper and is unable to manipulate facts to make them read like fiction. Nevertheless he claims that he is about to tell 'a shocking story – a tale of *real* horror' and warns anyone who 'can't stomach' such horror not to read on. We may be sceptical of the claim to factuality, but predictably we do read on, experiencing the action through Woodsley's eyes and like him wondering whether there is a rational explanation for the horrific events he encounters, or whether the accumulating horrors belong to the realms of the paranormal.

Eltonsbrody draws on several Gothic staples: an old house, from which the novel takes its title; a mysterious owner; locked rooms; mysterious past happenings; grisly relics; a rugged, inhospitable landscape; and ominously windy weather.[6] Mittelholzer locates his action precisely, in a setting that befits its remoteness from everyday realities. Eltonsbrody is situated in Barbados's 'Scotland district' on the island's wild Atlantic coast and, though it is only thirteen miles from the capital, Bridgetown, it is light years away from the seat of Barbados's civic institutions and the tourist beaches of its leeward Caribbean coast.

The central dynamic of the novel pivots on the relationship between Woodsley and Eltonsbrody's owner, Mrs Scaife, who welcomes him into her home as a non-paying guest and initially seems to be the epitome of a kindly old lady. Woodsley is gradually disabused of this view of her, as apparent horrific events proliferate. He tries to tell himself he may be the butt of a bizarre practical joke and her grim humour provides grounds for such a belief, but he is gradually forced into realizing that her superficial benevolence belies a very different strain in her character. She openly admits to experiencing schadenfreude when thinking of the death of others and claims to have a psychic gift that enables her to recognize those with 'the Mark' (an attraction to the macabre) and those with 'the Shadow' (people who are about to die). She tells Woodsley that he bears the Mark, which is in keeping with his own admission that he has 'a distinctly sinister mien'. He is the outsider who comes into the eerie Gothic world of Eltonsbrody by chance, he doesn't share Mrs Scaife's joy in horror, and he is repelled by the more gruesome aspects of her words and deeds, but nevertheless he has affinities with her. At the end of his narrative, when his worst suspicions have been confirmed, he still feels a degree of empathy for Mrs Scaife and wants to keep an open mind on her character. So, although he does not act out his own 'dark' fantasies, his attraction to the macabre, which Mrs Scaife quickly detects, makes him a kindred spirit to her.

Woodsley is fairly obviously a fictional *alter ego* for his creator, but in the view of Jacqueline Ives, Mittelholzer's second wife, Mrs Scaife also reflects traits in his own psychic make-up: his 'obsession with death' and his 'fascination with the dark, the weird and the strange'.[7] There is nothing new in using the Gothic to probe aberrant mental states – founding Gothic texts such as William Godwin's *Caleb Williams* and Mary Shelley's *Frankenstein* do just this – but, that said, the bizarre psychology that underpins *Eltonsbrody* has a flavour all of its own. It is Mittelholzer's achievement that, through the medium of Woodsley's narrative, he is able to bring Mrs Scaife's worldview alive and strike a balance between seeing it as inhumanly repugnant and, taking her at her own estimate, as a source of grim humour. Woodsley ends his account saying, 'The very name Eltonsbrody seems like a ragged, sticky piece of cobweb that will cling for all time round the nerve-cells of my brain' and many of the book's readers will find that it lingers long in *their* minds after they have put the novel down.

JOHN THIEME

JOHN THIEME is a Senior Fellow at the University of East Anglia. He previously held Chairs at the University of Hull and London South Bank University, and has also taught at the Universities of Guyana and North London. His books include *Postcolonial Con-Texts: Writing Back to the Canon*, *Postcolonial Literary Geographies: Out of Place*, the novel *The Book of Francis Barber*, and studies of Derek Walcott, V.S. Naipaul and R.K. Narayan.

Further Reading

Brown, J. Dillon, *Migrant Modernism, Postwar London and the West Indian Novel*, Charlottesville and London: University of Virginia Press, 2013.

Gilkes, Michael, 'Edgar Mittelholzer', in *West Indian Literature*, ed. Bruce King, London and Basingstoke: Macmillan, 1979: 95-110.

Guckian, Patrick, 'The Balance of Colour – A Reassessment of the Work of Edgar Mittelholzer', *Jamaica Journal*, 4, 1 (1970): 38-45.

Ives, Jacqueline, *The Idyll and the Warrior*, 2012. http://www.prose-n-poetry.com/book_chapters/662.

Seymour, A.J. 'The Novels of Edgar Mittelholzer', *Kyk-over-al*, 8, 24 (1958): 60-74.

Thieme, John, 'Catching Mullet and Chasing Shadows: The Early Novels of Edgar Mittelholzer', *Caribbean Review*, 8, 4 (1979): 36-37 and 47-50.

Westmaas, Juanita Anne, *Edgar Mittelholzer (1909-1965) and the Shaping of His Novels*, PhD thesis, University of Birmingham, 2013. http://etheses.bham.ac.uk/4367.

NOTES

1   His experimental novels *Latticed Echoes* (1960) and *Thunder Returning* (1961) make extensive use of a Wagnerian leit-motiv technique, introducing this into stories which are otherwise told entirely in dialogue.

2   *Children of Kaywana* (1952), *The Harrowing of Hubertus* (1954; also published as *Hubertus* and *Kaywana Stock*) and *Kaywana Blood* (1958; also published as *The Old Blood*).

3   Jacqueline Ives, *The Idyll and the Warrior*, Chapter 8. http://www.prose-n-poetry.com/display_work/21671.

4   A.J. Seymour, 'The Novels of Edgar Mittelholzer', *Kyk-over-al*, 8, 24 (1958), 70.

5   The name suggests an authorial self-projection. Mittelholzer appears to have chosen it as an English equivalent of the third syllable of his own surname: 'holz' is the German for wood. He had already used it in *My Bones and My Flute* (1955), where the protagonist is named Milton Woodsley, and his novel *The Mad MacMullochs* (1959) had been published under the pseudonym H. Austin Woodsley.

6   Weather figures prominently in much of Mittelholzer's fiction, e.g., *Corentyne Thunder* (1941), *The Weather Family* (1952), *The Weather in Middenshot* (1958), *Thunder Returning* (1961) and *The Piling of Clouds* (1961). In his early life, he worked as a meteorologist in Georgetown, Guyana. Jacqueline Ives, *The Idyll and the Warrior*, Introduction – 1. http://www.prose-n-poetry.com/display_work/21639.

7   Jacqueline Ives, *The Idyll and the Warrior*, Chapter 10. http://www.prose-n-poetry.com/display_work/22356.

I

I HAVE READ MANY HORROR STORIES, factual and fictional. In the fictional ones, I have noticed, the author generally manipulated things so that his readers could feel cosily certain that in the end all would come well with the virtuous and upright protagonists. Despite the turgidly harrowing atmosphere, despite the nasty black horror threatening everyone, the Right People would emerge safe and sound, the Wrong People would get their comeuppance. I wish it were something like that I was sitting down to write now—but it's not. This thing I am about to record could make a really terrifying fictional horror story, and if I were a good journalist (or, better, a novelist) I would be able to colour it up nicely and put in a lot of meaty thrills, and I would be able to arrange matters so that the Virtuous and the Upright were left in the end not only safe and intact but happily poised for the sound of wedding-bells.

Unfortunately, I am a commercial artist (and landscape painter for my own amusement). I can handle colour on a canvas but not colour in words on paper. I am no good whatever at manipulating facts so as to make them read like convincing fiction, so I shall have to content myself with the Bare Facts. It's a shocking story—a story of *real* horror—and anyone who feels that he can't stomach *real* horror had better go no further than here. For those who feel they're up to it, well, let's be off!

It was on the fourth night of my stay at Eltonsbrody that things, so to speak, began to dip the wrong way. In answer to a light knock, I opened my bedroom door and saw the old lady, Mrs. Scaife. She was standing in the corridor with a lamp. It was the lamp I had seen on the table beside her bed in her own room. Her room was on the same side of the house as mine, and, in fact, adjoined mine, though there was no connecting door. She was in her olive-green dressing-gown, a smallish, slim person, partially grey, with a mild face but alert, practical-looking pale-blue eyes.

'Has anything disturbed you to-night, Mr. Woodsley?' she asked.

'No. Nothing at all,' I said. 'Why?'

My voice and manner were surprised and wondering, but she gave no sign of being aware of this. Her air was as casual as though it might have been nine in the morning instead of nearly eleven at night.

She smiled. 'In that case I'll be going to bed.' She glanced past me into the room. 'You seem to have been reading.'

'Trying to—by lamplight. Not good, though. Straining my eyes.'

'Yes, you shouldn't read by lamplight. The wind doesn't disturb you, does it? It seems unusually strong to-night.'

'Just as usual to me. Seems to have been blowing like the dickens from the instant I topped the cliff three evenings ago. Does it ever get calm on this side of the island?'

'Sometimes—but very rarely.'

'Is there anything wrong, Mrs. Scaife?'

'Wrong?'

'Yes. I mean, what do you think could have disturbed me to-night? You didn't come last night to ask me if anything was wrong—nor the two nights before.'

She did not lose her composure. 'You're certainly blunt, Mr. Woodsley. It's a good trait. I like bluntness.'

I laughed. 'Everybody won't agree with you. Some people dislike me for my bluntness.'

She smiled. 'I suppose so. My husband, Michael, was much like you so far as bluntness goes. I think it indicates a probing mind. Most forthright people have probing minds. Well, good night—and I'm glad you haven't been troubled by anything.'

'Good night, Mrs. Scaife—and I hope I won't be.'

Going back to the easy chair by the window, I said to myself that had she been a young woman I would in no way have been puzzled over the incident. Indeed, I should have thought it perfectly understandable, and would even have been half-expecting it, for my vanity knows no limit, and she and I were alone in this big house, she the mistress and I her guest—and not a paying guest, either.

She had taken me in for the very simple reason that I had found myself stranded (if that is not too strong a word) in this part of the island. I had travelled here from Bridgetown on the chance that I would be able to secure a room at one of the two hotels. My fellow-boarders at the place I was staying had assured me that there would be no difficulty and it was a safe chance. But, on arrival, I found that the Easter holiday crowds had swamped every available room in both hotels. Even the little guesthouse called Shepherd's Rest House had been filled, and the time being a quarter to seven in the evening and no buses leaving for Bridgetown until the next morning, I would have had to choose between sleeping in the open air or on the veranda of one of the hotels (if permitted). The fisherfolk seemed to look upon me with suspicion, as though I might have been an agent sent by Mr. Khrushchev to investigate the possibilities of secret submarine bases in Barbados. I felt afraid to ask any of them for accommodation. (My face, I admit, is one that can easily excite suspicion in the most trusting strangers. I have deep-sunk eyes, heavy brows, a glum expression and, generally, a distinctly sinister mien).

It was the bus-driver who advised me to try Eltonsbrody, the big house on Staden. After hearing my tale of failure he said: 'Go up and try de big house you see yonder, chief. De ole lady, she's a koindly lady. She sure to help you out for de noight.'

He was more than right. Mrs. Scaife's face had become so lit up with pleasure on seeing me that I might have been a long-expected guest, or a beloved son or nephew who, after protracted travels, had, at last, returned to give her joy in her old age.

'How long are you in Barbados for?' she asked me. I told her a month.

'The first time you've come to this island?'

'The first time. I'm from England.'

'Oh, you're from England!'

'Well, actually, I was born in Antigua, but my parents took me to England when I was two years old. I grew up in England.'

'How long have you been in Barbados?'

'Five days to be exact. I arrived last Saturday. I'm staying a month.'

'Well, you must spend a week or two with me. This is the most beautiful part of the island—the Scotland District.'

'So I've heard. That's what has brought me this way. But I'm afraid too many other people thought the same, and the result is both the hotels, and even the resthouse, are crammed.'

'That's always the case at Easter. But never mind. I'm quite alone in this house. And strangers are always welcome, I'm sure.' She smiled as she added this, and it was a cordial, good-natured smile. There was nothing in it that could make me feel like a lonely wayfarer about to be murdered in his sleep.

We argued a bit over the question of my paying for board and lodging, but it was I who lost the argument (not that I minded losing), for she refused absolutely to accept a penny from me. I must believe her that it was a pleasure to have me. The house was so dull and empty that it was a relief when she could persuade anyone to stay. There was a room which was always kept prepared for guests, as her son, Mitchell, in Bridgetown, and her little grandson, sometimes came to spend a week-end. 'No, please don't let the matter of money trouble you for an instant, Mr. Woodsley. Just make yourself at home and stay as long as you like.'

So within less than fifteen minutes I was well installed in my room. And within half an hour I was sitting down to dinner, a meal Mrs. Scaife herself prepared, for the servants had all gone home, she explained. She apologised for the scanty meal (a fried flying fish, bread and butter and jam and a cup of cocoa), but added that, of course, she had not expected me and she herself never ate a heavy dinner. In fact, for dinner she never had more than a piece of flying fish, two slices of bread and a cup of tea. Anything heavier would have given her indigestion. She generally retired at half-past seven, and to fall asleep with an undigested meal on her stomach meant bad dreams and possibly vertigo the following morning. She dined punctually at six every evening.

Before this incident on the fourth night of my stay, there was nothing about Mrs. Scaife's behaviour, nothing in her speech or manner, to suggest that she might be flighty or in any way eccentric. She had treated me very well. At mealtime (I saw practically nothing of her at other times because I was always outdoors) she would ask me how I was enjoying myself, or how I liked the countryside, or had I climbed to the top of Bissex Hill yet?—just the ordinary, polite enquiries of a hostess eager to make her guest feel at home. Now and then, on direct prompting from me, she had told me about her late husband or her grandson, and had related a trifling incident of the past.

Through these conversations I learnt that Eltonsbrody was her own property, though it was entailed and would pass on to her son, Mitchell. She was the widow of Doctor Michael Scaife, a negro who had had a wide practice in this district and also, for some years, in Bridgetown and its environs thirteen miles away on the other side of the island. When her husband had died eight years before she had continued to live at Eltonsbrody, a well-off person whose only friends—or, for that matter, acquaintances of any sort—were her dogs and her servants. She herself was white—she came of Red Leg stock. The Red Legs are a small group of inbred whites, the descendants of the early Scottish-Irish settlers.

The tale of the gossips was (she told me this with an amused twinkle) that she had married Doctor Scaife for his money and he her for her white skin, and the argument was that the doctor had been such an ugly negro that even the women of his own race would not look at him twice, professional man though he was. And she, the daughter of lobster-fisher-folk in Martin's Bay, had been so ambitious for a better life and education that she had shut her eyes and said yes when the doctor met her at Bathsheba one Easter Monday and proposed. In actuality, she said, there was no truth in any of this. The marriage had resulted from a sincerely mutual fondness and a comradeship that had developed out of a similarity of outlook and ideas: 'the simpler human ideas, Mr. Woodsley—the plain, basic dreams and conceptions of two members of the same species.' Throughout married life, she assured me, relations between herself and her husband had been as harmonious and pleasant as it was within the capabilities of any human couple to achieve such a state.

Mitchell, the one child of their marriage, was a solicitor and a Member of the House of Assembly (the local Parliament). I gathered indirectly that he had fallen into disfavour with his mother a year after his father's death when he married a creole Portuguese girl from British Guiana. Or Trinidad (I am not sure which). With his family, he lived at a place called Bank Hall, a district on the outskirts of Bridgetown, and at irregular intervals ('any time he feels like it—I never try to persuade him') he came to Eltonsbrody to visit his mother, bringing with him his six-year-old son, Gregory. 'My grandson is the only interest I have in life, Mr. Woodsley.' Her eyes had become soft and doting when she said this. In fact, I got the impression that it was only because of Gregory that she tolerated Mitchell's visits. 'I happened to see the little fellow by accident when he was seven months old,' she told me, a faraway look in her eyes, 'and from that instant I knew he would always be very dear to me.'

I did not feel particularly sleepy, so sat staring out into the darkness of the casuarinas whose flimsy needle-like foliage kept wavering indistinctly against the starry sky. The wind zoomed and bellowed in monotonous fury round the house. Only subconsciously I heard it, for my senses had long grown accustomed to the sound. It was a sound that was never absent, for Staden (or as, I understand, it is more often called, Staden Hill) is one of the highest prominences in this north-eastern section of Barbados. Very rugged country it is—rugged and majestic. Austere, too. The very names of places have a bricky, stern sound. Hackleton's Cliff, Bissex Hill, Pico Teneriffe, Edgecombe Cliff. Only Bathsheba (where the two hotels and the rest-house are) falls with any softness on the ear.

For the most part of coralline limestone and clay, with ferruginous deposits, the land descends in whorled humps and tiers, studded with jagged, threatening boulders, to the narrow pebbly beach upon which the sea dashes itself minute after minute and hour after hour, every day, every week, with force and persistence.

Staden, where Eltonsbrody stands, though known as a hill, is, in actuality, a kind of plateau whose comparatively level top eventually slopes away in gentle undulations towards the south and west. On the seaward side it falls off rather steeply in desolate ledges and escarpments and occasional grass- or cane-grown patches down to the sea.

Eltonsbrody (where it got such a name from even Mrs. Scaife could not tell me) is a two-storeyed house with aged-looking grey limestone walls. It was built, if the date over the front door can be trusted, in 1887. Despite its isolation amid wide grounds bounded by patches of lonely canefields on the land side and the jagged descent on the sea side, Eltonsbrody, when I first saw it on that evening of Maundy Thursday, 1958, did not have a forbidding look. Rather it inspired something of the idyllic—and the trees that surrounded it were responsible for this: two or three mahogany trees, many tall, flimsy casuarinas—my favourite trees, incidentally, among all those I saw in the West Indies—and a few stunted flamboyants.

I had already decided that before I left I would transfer Eltonsbrody on to canvas, and I was thinking about the picture I had already started featuring the house when I heard the deep, brief bark of a dog. The sound came from the kitchen-garden, near the poultry-run, and I assumed it must be Walter.

The kennel was near the poultry-run, and Walter had just such a bark. He had Great Dane blood in him. Patrick was a mongrel.

I yawned, and was on the point of rising when I heard a rustle amid some shrubs which I knew grew along the path that led round the corner of the building to the driveway and the front garden. Somebody seemed to be walking along the path. I heard a chuckle. Mrs. Scaife's voice called up: 'Still not in bed yet, Mr. Woodsley? I'm going for a short walk.'

'A walk?'

'Yes. I'm not very sleepy to-night. I'm taking Walter and Patrick with me.'

'It's after eleven.'

'Oh, no harm will come to me. A short constitutional will help to induce sleep. It's an excellent habit to take walks before bed, my boy.'

I told myself it was no business of mine.

After I had put out the lamp and got into bed it suddenly came upon me that I was alone in Eltonsbrody. I admit I am imaginative and very susceptible to atmosphere. Lying there in bed, hearing the wind moaning and whooping round the house, I felt an eeriness descend upon me. Sounds that I had only a few minutes before taken for granted and accepted for what they were now took on a special significance. The soft swishing rustle of the casuarinas might have been a spirit-voice warning me of danger. And there was the old wardrobe in the room across the corridor that creaked occasionally. This creaking now seemed a sly, deliberate noise produced by some unknown presence that lurked behind the closed door of the unused room.

At this point I should explain about this room and about the other one that adjoined it, for it is important in view of what happened during the next few days.

There are five bedrooms at Eltonsbrody—two large ones on the windward side and two large ones on the leeward, with a corridor separating windward from leeward. The fifth room consists of a cut-off portion of the corridor. Instead of the corridor continuing right through to the eastern end of the building, a part of it had been walled in to make a small bedroom (there is a connecting door between this room and Mrs. Scaife's room which is one of the two on the leeward side). During the time of my stay, only the leeward rooms and this small room were in a fit state to be occupied. The two windward rooms were in disuse. The windows were kept closed and the doors were always locked (even though, as I came to learn later, they were both fully furnished). On the second day of my stay I happened to remark on this fact, and Mrs. Scaife told me with a sigh: 'This house is a real burden to me sometimes, Mr. Woodsley. I simply can't be bothered with those two rooms, and I think the servants have enough work as it is without having to keep clean two large rooms which nobody ever uses. You see, I have no friends—no friends at all. The people my son Mitchell would want to bring here are not the sort of people I'd like to know. I have no use for the artificial society in which Mitchell moves. I've always been a simple woman.'

A little later she explained about the wardrobe. It was the doctor's old wardrobe, and the base of one of the corner-supports was rotten, so that whenever a stray draught struck it the whole thing lurched a trifle and creaked.

And lying in bed now hearing it, I thought it sly and full of meaning—even found myself wondering if there could not be some sinister reason for those two rooms being locked up as they were.

I lit the lamp again and began to frown round the room. The walls were pale blue, and in places the plaster was flaked and cracked. The furniture was old-fashioned—except for the bed. Near the marble-topped washstand there hung a framed picture of the battle of Jutland. And just behind the bed, the smiling eyes of a girl of the rustic English type (circa 1880) gazed down upon me with sentimental persistence. The big four-sectioned wardrobe loomed along the eastern wall like a dark-brown monument saturated with Victorian austerity, and the chest of drawers that stood between the two southern windows had the air of a stout, corseted matron frowning in disapproval at the ultra-modernity of the Simmons bed.

Something made me spring up quickly and cross to the door. I opened the door a trifle, and listened.

After about a minute, the sound I had detected repeated itself, and my fears subsided. It was only the flapping of the piece of canvas sacking that Tappin, the man of all work, had hung out of the pantry window. The night before, I had come in late, and, in passing through the dining-room, had got quite a start on hearing this muffled flap-flap, like stealthy footsteps. I had investigated on the spot and solved the mystery.

I shut the door, and was turning to go back to bed when the telephone began to ring. The telephone was in Mrs. Scaife's room.

2

The obvious thing was to answer it, so I went in to answer it.

The door of her room was wide open (she kept it open all day). The big fourposter with tester and lace-frills dominated the scene. It had not been slept in for the night, I noticed. On a small table beside the bed the lamp was alight but turned low. It was on this table that the telephone stood. A male voice replied to my 'Hallo'. It sounded surprised, and wanted to know if this was Eltonsbrody.

'That's right,' I told it. 'I suppose you want to speak to Mrs. Scaife?' And it came back at me: 'Yes. Isn't she ... look here, would you mind telling me who you are?'

When I explained who I was and what I was doing here, he said: 'Oh,' and became quite affable, asked me if I was related to the Trinidad Woodsleys. I told him no, the Antigua Woodsleys, and he introduced himself as Mitchell Scaife. 'But where is Mother?' he wanted to know.

'Gone for a walk.'

'For a walk! At this hour!'

'I'm afraid so. Said she couldn't sleep. She's taking a constitutional. She's got the dogs with her.'

There was a pause while he seemed to consider something. Then in a voice become abruptly reserved, he said: 'Very well. I'll phone again later. Sorry to have disturbed you, Mr. Woodsley.'

'No need to worry about that. I was awake. Any message you'd like me to give her?'

A hesitation. Then: 'No, no,' he said. 'No, it's all right. I'll ring again later when I think she's returned home. Most unusual, her going out at this time of the night.'

'Our opinions coincide remarkably,' I murmured before hanging up.

The wardrobe in the doctor's room creaked, and the wind seemed to hum with a new mournfulness. I looked about the dimly lit room, and began to feel not too comfortable, as though I were being watched. I saw the door that opened into the small room, and found myself wondering what could be in there. Why had the corridor been cut off so that this room could be added to the four already in existence?

I turned up the lamp, very curious of a sudden. Was it my imagination or did the wind howl with a new fury as the light spilled redly round the room? I swore at myself for my fancifulness.

I took note of the wedge of wood that kept the door open. She only shut her door at night, but evidently to-night had brought a change in the routine. I shook my head and felt sure that something was wrong.

Though I had had many glimpses of her room from the corridor in passing, I had never come in here before. Looking round now, I saw nothing that might support the theory that my hostess was a person of eccentric habits. It was precisely the sort of room you might expect of an old lady like Mrs. Scaife. Neat, clean, smelling slightly of moth balls and lavender water, austere but restful and cosy. The big wardrobe and the easy chair by the window, the book-shelf over the wash-stand and the little table by the bed provided the cosiness.

Near the telephone on the bedside table I noticed what looked like a photograph album. I took it up and began to look through it. It was not one of these ponderous old-fashioned things. It was a modern snapshot album with accommodation for four small pictures on each page. All the pictures, I noticed, were of a child, and I took it for granted it must be her grandson, Gregory. This was confirmed on one page. Under one picture I read: 'Gregory, at two years.'

The pictures were in chronological order. The first four pictures on the first page showed Gregory as an infant recumbent, the second page showed him a little older; he was standing. Flicking through the pages, I watched him grow up to a little fellow of about six or seven.

I raised my head, listening.

No. Imagination. I could have sworn, though, I had heard a soft footstep in the corridor. Or could it have been in the small room? I put down the album and turned my gaze towards the connecting door. It was shut. I wanted to cross over and try it to see if it was locked. Was it a furnished room? What was kept in there? Had the sound of the footstep come from in there?

Only the wind seemed to know everything. I thought I could detect something intelligent in its whining drone—a cold, detached intelligence from which nothing in this dismal old house could hide. I could feel probing draughts twining round me, dissecting my thoughts—perhaps muttering inarticulate warnings that I was too stupid to catch and understand.

I had just glanced at the book-shelf when Mrs. Scaife's voice said: 'Having a look round, Mr. Woodsley?'

I started, of course—but in moments like this my nervous system has a peculiar habit of adjusting itself in a flash from shock to normality. The greater shock, it seems, the more abrupt the switchback to a state of presence of mind. I turned and smiled. 'Yes. I was glancing at this snapshot album of yours. I suppose it's Gregory, isn't it?'

She nodded, and advanced into the room in as silent-footed a manner as she must have come up the stairs and along the corridor. 'Yes, that is my dear little grandson. Didn't you notice his name under some of the pictures?'

'So I did.'

'He's much better to look at in real life. I'm sure there's no camera that can do him justice.'

'By the way, I haven't come in here out of inquisitiveness. Your son Mitchell phoned.'

She nodded again. 'I was expecting the call.'

'You were?'

'Yes. And, please, Mr. Woodsley, you must never consider it inquisitive to come in here. You're always welcome. I have nothing to hide.'

I thanked her, then said: 'You say you were expecting this phone call. Then why did you go out?'

She took up the photograph-album. 'I should have thought the reason was obvious. I wanted to be out when the phone rang.'

I stared at her.

'Did he say if he'd ring again?'

'He did. He said he'd call later—I don't know how late that means. But, like myself, he was a bit puzzled at your going for a walk at this time of the night.'

Her manner vaguely abstracted, she asked: 'Were you puzzled, too?'

It might have been the heightened state of my fanciful-ness—or it might have been the draught that swirled through the room at this instant—but I shuddered. And I thought that there was something in her voice very peculiar. She somehow made her words sound weighted with menace and prophecy; yet, at the same time, there was a sympathetic note some-where in it. Yet sympathetic in a way that revolted me. It was just as though she had not a moment ago committed a disgusting act, and now was whispering to me: 'Why do you pretend to be puzzled? Aren't we both in the same category?'

'Of course I was puzzled,' I replied, a little resentfully. 'Who wouldn't be puzzled at your behaviour? Going for a walk at eleven o' clock at night when you knew your son would be ringing you up. Very puzzling I call it. Anyway, it's your business. What right have I to criticise you!'

I began to move towards the door, but she said quickly: 'You're such a hasty young man. So hasty and plain-spoken! Please don't hurry off. Won't you like to look through my book-shelf? When I came in you appeared to be interested in it. Don't hesitate if there's anything you see and think you'd like to borrow.' She spoke with a touch of anxiety—almost ingratiatingly, as though the last thing she wanted to do was to offend me.

I paused and said: 'As a matter of fact, I'd barely glanced at your books when you appeared like a ghost at the door.'

'Yes, I did move silently. A habit of mine sometimes. Never mind, my boy. Indulge me. Come and have a closer look at my books.'

I moved over to the book-shelf, and she took up the lamp and brought it. As she stood behind me I thought I sensed something breathless about her. She seemed in some peculiar way rigid with excitement. Or perhaps anxiety would be the better word. It made me very uncomfortable, though I tried not to show it.

'All these books were given to me by my husband during our courting days.' she said. 'With the exception of one.'

I opened my mouth to ask: 'Which one?' but changed my mind.

My gaze took in titles like *Tanglewood Tales, Human Anatomy, Lamb's Essays, Origin of Species, Pilgrim's Progress, Royal Reader No. V* . . .

She seemed to divine the trend of my thoughts, for she remarked: 'An odd collection, isn't it? But every one is a dear friend. It was through these books that I learnt of the world and its sophistries. These books and my husband were my only tutors.' She spoke with a certain pride, with a deep affection, too, her manner getting a trifle vacant. She uttered low, reminiscent grunts. Old-lady grunts.

I turned and asked: 'What's in that room over there—the small room? Is it a disused room, too, like the windward ones?'

'That? No. Oh, no,' she told me. 'That's where Gregory stays when he comes here to see me.' She moved towards the connecting door and beckoned me to follow her. And during the next few minutes I saw how absurd it is to let one's imagination get the better of one. For there was nothing whatever sinister about this little room. I saw a small bed, with a table beside it on which stood an old-fashioned portable gramophone and an album of records (all 78's by the look of them)—I thumbed through the album casually. There was a clothes-cupboard which she opened so that I could see the contents: tiny trousers and shirts and what looked like a miniature cricket cap.

'I always keep a clean supply of clothes ready for him,' she said. 'It saves his parents the bother of having to pack for him when he comes to spend a week-end with me.' She wagged her head and sighed—then suddenly stiffened.

The telephone began to ring.

I felt her hand on my wrist. 'Don't answer it.'

'But . . .'

'Let it ring until it stops.'

'But it must be your son. Mitchell.'

'I'm aware of that. Mitchell is the only person who puts through telephone calls to this house.' Her grip on my wrist tightened. I could sense the breathlessness in her manner.

The wind whined round the eaves.

'Mr. Woodsley, have you ever felt overcome by both horror and joy at the same time?'

I shook my head. I made an attempt to return into the other room, but she stayed me. 'Please. Let's remain in here for a moment, if you don't mind. I know my behaviour must seem strange, but bear with me, my boy.' I could feel her trembling.

I indulged her, and we stood there, listening to the wind—and the ringing of the telephone. Every now and then a chilly draught curled round my ankles or twined clammy tentacles about my neck.

After a moment I could not help murmuring: 'Very strange behaviour.'

A shaky chuckle came from her. 'Michael was just as volatile and blunt as you are—but he was tolerant, too. Yes, he was always considerate of my whims. I'm not a bad woman, Mr. Woodsley—but I'm strange. Strange in a strange way.'

The wind continued to drum round the building like a live, frustrated creature outside in the dark. The telephone continued to ring.

'Strange in a way not one of my fellow creatures would dream possible. But I'm not bad. Nor am I insane. You must never be afraid of me.' She uttered an exclamation of impatience. 'Why doesn't he put down the phone! Can't he realise by now I'm not going to answer it?'

Her hand with the lamp trembled so much that I thought it wise to relieve her. I took the lamp and advised her to be calm.

Suddenly the phone grew silent, and she relaxed. She smiled and said with a sigh: 'That's much better. I thought he would never give up.'

As we moved back into her own room I remarked: 'If this is a game, I think it a bit unfair that you should keep me in the dark.'

She patted my shoulder in a motherly manner, and smiled. 'Don't you like mysteries? Don't tell me you don't. All humans do.'

'I must be the unique exception. I detest mysteries. Especially in houses like this which possess, so to speak, all the accessories for weird and ghostly phenomena.'

'No, you only say that to sound clever. Search your heart and you'll find I'm right. The perplexing always appeals to people, and I'm certain you're no exception. You see, I can be plain-spoken, too.' She wagged a playful finger at me.

I shrugged and bade her good night, and as I was going out she called after me: 'Would you care to go for a walk with me in the morning after breakfast?'

'No objections at all,' I said. 'Hope it won't be too far, though, because I want to do a bit of painting before the sun gets too high.'

'Yes, you did mention it at dinner. You want to do a picture of the house, you said.'

'That's right.'

'Well, you need have no fear. I don't intend to go very far. Half a mile or so. I'm taking you to the cemetery.'

3

I am not religious. That is why I avoided Morning Prayers. These were conducted by Mrs. Scaife before breakfast in the dining-room, and four of the five servants had to be present, the fifth, McTurk, the poultry-man, having insisted on being an absentee on the grounds that he had too much work to do in the morning.

As on the previous mornings, I reclined in my easy chair (the one I had selected as my favourite) in the large sitting-room while I waited for the performance to come to an end.

There was no dividing wall between sitting-room and dining-room. Four fluted pillars with Corinthian capitals marked the boundary, so to speak, between the two rooms, and from my easy chair I commanded an unhindered view of everything going on in the dining-room.

The walls of the sitting-room were dark-brown and varnished, giving the atmosphere in here a restfulness and dignity rather than gloom. The furniture was Victorian—heavy, ornate, carved table-legs, what-nots, a mantelpiece with a mirror, a sofa, rocking-chairs. The easy chair in which I sat had once been an armchair, erect and prim, but, on Mitchell's request, two years before, it had been remodelled and modernised by Tappin, the man-of-all-work. Three huge lithographs in black frames depicting mass scenes by Gustav Doré decorated the northern, eastern and western walls (there was no southern wall; where the southern wall should have been the fluted columns stood), one to each wall, and below each, like acolytes in attendance on a priest, hung two sepia landscape scenes in gold frames—cows and misty mountains and trees; and deer and misty mountains and trees; and sheep and misty mountains and trees; distant cows, water, misty mountains and trees.

Wearing her olive-green dressing-gown and with her Bible, a small one in worn morocco leather, Mrs. Scaife came downstairs and took her place near the old, heavy, carved, mahogany sideboard. And as though they had divined her advent by some psychic means, the servants entered from the pantry and began to range themselves round the room.

Tappin, the man-of-all-work, posted himself under a big picture of Doctor Scaife. He was a heavily built, lumbering negro, and had a permanent bloodshot mark on the white of his left eye that, somehow, gave him a certain attractiveness when he smiled, though when he was serious or dismayed it could look repulsive—even grotesque.

Jackman, the cook, a thin, tall negress, took up a position near a southern window so that she could surreptitiously watch (so I discovered later) the kitchen and tell by the smoke from the chimney whether the fire she had lit for heating water for coffee was 'going down or keeping up.'

Malverne, the housemaid, an anaemic-looking Red Leg girl with a remarkably good figure, stood very primly, her hands clasped before her, between the picture of Mr. Gladstone and the one of Edward VII.

Bayley, the yard-boy and messenger, stood right under Edward VII. He was the only one of the four of them, it appeared, who had not fallen into the habit of taking up a regular position at Morning Prayers. He was a boy of about fifteen, and one whose portrait I was determined to paint before I left Eltonsbrody. He had a dull, moronic expression that could alter with startling suddenness to one of intelligence and mischief, and his costume consisted of an old cream-coloured waistcoat worn over an orange (sometimes pink or green) sports-shirt. This waistcoat—so Jackman had told me—he slept in at night as well as wore during the day. It only left his person on the occasion of his twice-a-week bath and on Sundays when he changed it for a dark-green one. Both waistcoats, Jackman had said, had once been the property of Doctor Scaife.

Morning prayers took the form of a reading of the Scriptures as dictated by the Book of Common Prayer (Mrs. Scaife was Anglican, and had, in fact, met Doctor Scaife at a bazaar meeting at the Rectory of St. Joseph's Church which is not far from Eltonsbrody).

This morning, she told them, the First Lesson was from Joshua, the Second from Luke. She never, it seemed, quoted chapter and verse.

She read the Lessons in an expressive and distinct voice, and I could not help thinking that she would have made a very successful wireless announcer. Lowering the Bible after she had read the Lessons, she bowed her head, and the others bowed theirs, too.

'Our Father,' she began, and the servants joined in from 'which art in heaven.' The sound of their voices saying the Lord's Prayer made a murmurous rumble throughout the room, creating perfect harmony, I thought, with the persistent droning of the wind past the house and the subdued flapping of the piece of canvas sacking that Tappin had hung out of the pantry window the afternoon before. (To this day I have not discovered to what use this sacking was put). The bleating of a goat from the pens beyond the poultry-run might have been an upsetting note, but it was too remote. The wind muffled it and wafted it off into the mahogany trees whose foliage kept up their soft background lisping.

They had got as far as 'and forgive us our trespasses' when the accident of the picture happened.

I heard a scraping whisk and thud and a cry. It was Malverne who cried out. Bayley started back with a gasp and a loud 'Oi!', his face blank and idiotic.

It was the picture of Mr. Gladstone. It lay, face down, on the floor, two or three triangular pieces of glass pushing out from under the heavy brown frame. The thick, dusty cord at the back had snapped.

Tappin advanced towards it slowly, with a lumbering caution. His left eye with the bloodshot mark seemed to me positively baleful. 'But how dat happen?' he said in a perplexed voice.

Bayley looked at me as I approached. He grinned. 'Sir, ef Oi didn't move it woulda hit me,' he said.

'Naturally,' I replied.

Mrs. Scaife was smiling at me.

Then Tappin began to pick up the fallen picture. 'Miss Dahlia, dis is a bad soign,' he said, shaking his head. 'A very bad soign.'

His mistress glanced at him sharply. Her smile had vanished. She snapped: 'What? What's that? A bad sign?'

'Yes, Miss Dahlia. A very bad soign. It mean somebody going to dead.'

'Oh, shut up! Shut up! What utter nonsense!'

They all glanced at her in surprise. I myself was a bit taken aback at this display of anger. And anger it was. She glared at Tappin, her face pale, her hand clutched tight round the Bible.

Tappin stared at her in dismay.

'Death! Death! It means that somebody is going to die. Why should you be so morbid, man? Can't you see it's an accident? Look at the cord! It's rotten. Look, Mr. Woodsley! Look!' She turned towards me, her manner anxious, agitated. 'Please convince this superstitious idiot that there's no reason to come to gruesome conclusions because a picture has fallen from the wall!' She snatched the picture from Tappin. 'See! Look at the cord! Worn and rotten!' She held the cord and jerked it between her fingers. It snapped. 'See that!' She looked at me in triumph. 'Absolutely no good. It snapped from sheer age. Yet this fool wants to make out that it's a sign of death!'

Abruptly I said: 'But many people do consider it a sign of death when a picture falls from the wall, Mrs. Scaife. Even in England.'

She looked at me and stiffened. 'What do you mean, Mr. Woodsley? Are you—do you mean to tell me you're going to support this—this country lout in his superstitious beliefs?'

I was in no way put out. I chuckled and said: 'I'm afraid, Mrs. Scaife, that I can't agree with you that the superstition is limited only to country louts. I know a great number of people—civilised town-folk in England—who not only take seriously the falling-picture superstition but even believe in such omens as the smashed mirror and the hooting of an owl outside a window. Not only peasants in Barbados.'

She stared at me for an instant, baffled, then asked: 'Do you mean that *you* believe in these absurd superstitions?'

'I never said so. I believe in only what my reason can encompass. But all the same, I feel you're being rather unfair to this fellow. I can't see any need for you to get so worked up over a trivial incident like this. What's the matter, Mrs. Scaife? Even if he does feel it's a sign of death why should you be so upset? If you consider it absurd, then why not shrug your shoulders and forget the matter? Why make a scene?'

This I knew, was going a bit far, and I had expected to be sharply snubbed. But she did not snub me. She uttered a nervous, jerky sound and turned off, murmuring: 'You're perfectly right, Mr. Woodsley. I'm making a fuss about nothing, really.' She handed the picture back to Tappin. 'You may have this mess cleaned up, Tappin. And please get a new piece of glass fitted back in this picture.'

'Yes, Miss Dahlia,' he said, his dismay merging into relief.

His mistress smiled and told him: 'I'm afraid my behaviour must have startled you, Tappin. Well, never mind! I didn't sleep very well last night. Put it down to that.'

A little later, when she and I were sitting down to breakfast at the long, ponderous dining-table capable of accommodating well over a dozen people, I said to her: 'Something is on your mind, Mrs. Scaife. Even at the risk of seeming officious, I'm going to express the opinion that you're worried.'

She smiled. 'I have already told you, Mr. Woodsley, that you must never consider it officious to express any opinion concerning myself and my affairs. I welcome it—welcome it sincerely. Yes, I admit I am worried. I meant to tell you of it when we go for our walk.' Suddenly she became a little dreamy in manner. She began to smile to herself as she unfolded her napkin, as though musing upon some matter that called forth both her sorrow and her delight.

I waited for her to go on, wondering whether she could be sane.

Without looking up, she said: 'I know you're thinking me a lunatic, but please don't attach too much importance to my behaviour this morning—nor last night. Do you remember something I said last night?' She looked at me. 'Horror and joy, Mr. Woodsley. Have you ever found yourself in the grip of both at once?'

The question was not rhetorical, so I shook my head and replied: 'No. And I can't see how it's possible for anyone to be both horrified and joyful at one and the very same time.'

She sat forward at once, her eyes on me—eager, alive. 'I know! Oh, I know! Perfectly right, my boy. That's why I mentioned it. It's so remarkable. But that's just how I feel. I'm overjoyed and yet I'm horrified and depressed. I know it sounds quite mad, and many times I've questioned my own sanity, too. The doctor has often done that, but he was tolerant and understanding. That's why we got on so well.'

She put down her knife and fork, shifted in her chair with a sort of feverishness, her gaze steady on me. 'I may as well tell you, I'm—' she hesitated—'I'm not what we might call an ordinary person. Perhaps before you leave I may tell you about it, because you, somehow, inspire me with a feeling of trust.

In many ways, you're identically like the doctor. Not black and ugly. No, you're very handsome. But I mean plain-spoken and—and lacking in hypocrisy. I wish Mitchell were like you. We might have been closer. As it is, I despise him heartily. He's simply another tissue hypocrite of a politician and a society figure-head! All he can talk about is this stupid federation of the West Indies and the people he had cocktails with at Government House. Tch, tch! But there! I'm getting worked up again!' She sighed and relaxed, and began to pick at the bacon rashers in her plate.

I kept observing her quietly as I ate.

'I do so like simple, straightforward people,' she began to mumble, half to herself. I could see that she was making a great effort to control herself, but even though she spoke in a mumble there was a quivering intensity in her manner. 'God must have sent you to me, Mr. Woodsley. You're the first person I've felt like confiding in since the doctor died.' Her gaze had strayed past me to the sideboard.

The sun was thrusting slanted pointers into the room. Filtered as it was through the foliage of the casuarinas, the sunshine made shifty, rib-like patterns on the walls and on the draped part of the cloth that covered the sideboard.

'It's strange how the imagination can convert the ordinary into the significant,' she said quietly. 'When one's mind, for instance, is centred on the subject of death everything seems to conspire to reveal the presence of the Gaunt Spectre. Look at that sunlight playing on the walls. I can see dancing skeletons in those patterns. Notice the rib-like formation?'

'Why should your mind be centred on the subject of death?' I asked.

She shrugged. 'Well, why shouldn't it, my boy? I think we should all keep our minds centred on the subject of death. It's the one exciting event we can every one of us look forward to experiencing—and look forward with the absolute certainty that we won't be disappointed.'

I made no comment, and after a silence she went on: 'Take

that picture falling. I was perfectly aware of the superstition, but it irritated me to hear that black fool saying it so confidently. It was the last thing I'd wanted to hear—at the moment. Poor Tappin. I gave him a scare. We're such good friends. I don't think I've scolded him for years. I love my servants, Mr. Woodsley. Even McTurk, grouchy as he is. They've been with me for years—and Tappin is a good man. He may look odd, what with that cast in his eye, but he's a versatile fellow. A good gardener, a good carpenter, a good joiner, a reliable messenger. He goes to town to do my shopping every Wednesday and Saturday. My God! Look! Look at that!'

I turned my head.

She was pointing at a large clump of brain coral. It was the most prominent object on the sideboard. It loomed there like a mountain, greyish and convoluted and pitted, surrounded by the glassware—large flasks and mugs and jugs and decanters and tumblers.

'What's the matter?' I asked.

'A worm moved in that coral.'

'A worm?'

'A worm of decay. A maggot.'

'What are you talking about?'

'Another sign of death—at least, so the superstitious would say.' She gave a brief, nervous laugh. 'Only an illusion created by a stray sun-beam, of course, my boy. But it gave me a start. In my present mood, everything seems significant. Every commonplace phenomenon holds in it the indication of either life or death.'

I put down my knife and fork. 'Now, look here,' I said, 'let's get this clear, Mrs. Scaife. Why this reference to death? Are you expecting anyone in here to die?'

I saw her hand tremble, saw her eyes grow shifty, but in an instant she had regained control of herself. She smiled and shrugged. 'We must always be expecting someone to die. No, no! Please don't explode. I'm speaking evasively on purpose to tease you. I do like to have my little fun sometimes, you

know.' She shook her head and hurried on: 'No, I can't say
honestly I'm expecting any deaths in this house—unless, of
course, they are deaths that occur by accident. Ah, yes, if you
mean it that way, then I may tell you that I am always expecting someone in here to fall and hurt himself fatally—or take
poison unwittingly in his food. There's the housemaid, for
instance—Malverne. She's an eccentric girl—in various ways.
Rather embarrassing ways, as you may discover before long.
And she's dyspeptic. Suffers from giddy spells. I'm always
warning her to be careful when going home in the evening.
The path down to Martin's Bay is very steep at certain points.
If she were to be attacked by a giddy spell one evening and
fell . . .' She shrugged, leaving the sentence unfinished. Then
she smiled at me—with genuine good humour, and with an
irony which seemed to denote her complete awareness of
what I was thinking about her.

'Has she approached you at any time?'

'Approached me? What do you mean?'

She shrugged and sighed. 'Never mind, never mind.'

'But I'm interested. Do you mean she—ah—well, you
know what I mean!' I felt the blood in my face.

She chuckled teasingly. 'You're blushing. Very well. Since
you're curious. She's something of a problem-girl. Sexually.
She doesn't look it, I know, but it's there under her innocent
mien.'

Fidgeting, I asked: 'What precise form does it take?'

'I think the term generally used is—exhibitionist. But let's
not go into that now. I can see you're embarrassed in spite of
your curiosity.'

I didn't press the matter, and after a silence she said: 'If you
go upstairs and look on my book-shelf—I'm not telling you
to do so, mind!—you'll find there a volume that might shock
you. It would tell you many astounding and horrifying things.
It's not a printed book. It's a loose-leaf manuscript enclosed
within the covers of a book. When I came in last night and
found you staring at my book-shelf I was a little alarmed. But

there, there! I'm a talkative old woman. My tongue will get me into serious trouble before long.'

I said nothing.

Around us the house seemed to vibrate in the unceasing drone of the wind outside. Now and then a window in the sitting-room would rattle faintly like a voice sounding in the throat of a dying person.

Presently Mrs. Scaife broke the silence that had come upon us. She began to talk about her kitchen garden. The weather was very dry at present, and her celery was suffering. And her poor eddoes looked quite yellowish. But the lettuce was doing well. Suddenly she sighed and said: 'But what do a few plants matter? Human life is much more important. But what does life mean? And what is death? Even you, my boy, don't realise that robust and vital as you may feel yourself to be, the mark of death is strong on your cheek.'

4

When I asked her for an explanation of this remark she smiled and murmured sententiously: 'To some of us it is given to see, my boy. Others must be blind. But we have to go for our walk, haven't we? I mustn't keep you here with my baffling remarks. Let me go upstairs and get ready.'

A few minutes later as we set out in a southerly direction along the main motor road, she told me that going for a walk was nothing out of the ordinary for her. Perhaps two or three times a week she would take Walter and Patrick and stroll down to Martin's Bay or to Bathsheba. Or she might go in the opposite direction, as we were doing now, and get as far as the old windmill near Horse Hill. Morning, she said, was always her time for walking. She never went out in the afternoon or evening.

'So I take it, last night's outing was due to sheer whim?' I spoke in an indulgent voice.

'No, it was no whim. I think I told you I went out because I wanted to avoid being in the house when the phone rang. I'm a mystifying person, Mr. Woodsley. I can see you're curious and intrigued. Well, never mind. Who doesn't like a mystery? Be frank now, my boy. Doesn't it add spice to your stay at Eltonsbrody, these queer antics I've begun to indulge in?'

'Am I to understand that your queer antics are being performed to provide me with entertainment?'

'No, I wouldn't say that. It's simply that you're fortunate to have arrived here at this particular time. But let's not go into the matter any further. I'm interested in you, Mr. Woodsley—very interested. And I have an idea that before we part company you'll be a far more enlightened young man in the strangeness of this world.'

She halted and pointed down at Martin's Bay. Down there, she told me, in a tiny shingled cottage, she had been born sixty-odd years ago. Down there, too, she went on, was the Well Pit where boats were sometimes sucked down with the men in them. It was a deep crevasse in the rocks no more than ten yards wide but of a depth that had never been fathomed. The sea boiled over the spot continuously, and during the day you could see the water there, dark blue-green. A dark blue-green patch amid the rest of greenish water, edged with foam and a few jutting rocks. That was your only way of knowing the spot from a distance in daytime, though the fisherfolk of Martin's Bay, not to mention herself, could tell where it was even at midnight. Yes, she herself could go down this rugged hillside to Martin's Bay at any time, in the dark, and lead me to the spot, tell me in what direction to swim to reach the deathly whirlpool. It was not far from the beach. A short, brisk swim— and then down, down, down, never to come up.

I listened to her, making no comment, but missing nothing. Those rocks down there, she said, were part of her bone-frame. The salt air was in her breath—and the wind with its smell of iodine, and, sometimes, of fish. Her girlhood days in Martin's Bay had left a stamp on her that would never be erased, no matter if she lived to ninety or a hundred. The education she had garnered in the elementary village school, and then the greater wealth of learning that she had devoured during the two years that Doctor Scaife had courted her and helped her to become acquainted with books and the affairs of the world outside this small island, the knowledge of men and their vileness that she had drunk in during her early married years, all that—yes, even that could not crush out the deep mark of those days when, as an ignorant but alert and imaginative girl, she would stand on the beach at night and watch her father and brothers wading out amid the rocks with lighted torches to catch lobsters and crabs and cuttlefish.

We had got now far past the canefields that stretched southward from the grounds of Eltonsbrody. She turned off the main road into a track that descended into a gully. Soon, however, we were ascending again along a more well-defined path that meandered through coarse, drought-afflicted grass.

A few minutes later we came out upon another highway, and going down-hill now and in a north-easterly direction, we soon came within sight of the cemetery she had mentioned the night before. This cemetery, she explained, was owned by a group of white planter-families of the district. Only members of their own families and very close friends were buried here.

'But,' she went on, pride in her voice, 'it is here Michael was buried. He was the first negro, and the only one, to be buried on this land, Mr. Woodsley—and I can assure you, neither Mitchell nor I asked permission for this privilege. Of their own free wills the heads of the four families sent and requested that the doctor be buried on their land here. Oh, yes. They respected Michael—loved and respected him. Both white and black. I don't think there was a man more beloved in this island. That he should have been laid to rest in this select and reserved little cemetery is no surprise. It was his due.' She spoke with emotion, with a deep earnestness and pride.

The descent into the cemetery was sharp and steep. When

we got to the bottom of the declivity she paused and said: 'We need go no further. Here is Michael's tomb.'

It was one of three on the outskirts of the little cemetery— a simple, ungarnished tomb of concrete, painted white. Every six months, she informed me, she had it painted anew. The inscription engraved on it was, also, very simple:

> DOCTOR MICHAEL SCAIFE
> Born 9th December, 1885
> Died 12th January, 1950
> A MAN

'Yes, Mr. Woodsley. A man. In every sense, a man. One of the best men that ever lived.'

The wind rustled softly amidst the grass around the tombs. It was the only sound in the stillness. A dryish, limestone smell and a vague dankness pervaded the air.

Suddenly a sound other than that of the wind in the grass began to obtrude. It seemed to be a low moaning. I saw Mrs. Scaife's head come up, alert and eager. Her body grew tensed, and her hands clenched slowly.

The inclination to glance about came upon me. Then I felt like an utter fool. My silly fancy again magnifying things and making everything appear weird! It was the drone of a motor. On the road above us, laden with canes, a lorry came into view. For an instant it seemed about to plunge down upon us, then it swung round the sharp bend and disappeared beyond a canefield to the northeast of the cemetery where the road dipped steeply towards Martin's Bay.

I noticed that Mrs. Scaife's eyes were gleaming in a peculiar way. She looked at me and murmured: 'I wonder if the same thought passed through your mind as passed through mine, my boy?'

I felt myself shuddering. It was like the night before when, standing near me with that photograph-album, she had asked me if I were puzzled. In her voice was that same note of something prophetic, of something sympathetic, as though, perhaps, I were an accomplice of hers in some terrible deed she had done or were about to do.

I said curtly: 'I'm quite sure not. Nothing passed through my mind. Nothing at all.'

She smiled. 'It's no use pretending, Mr. Woodsley. You know as well as I do that the figure of Death hovered over our shoulders for one tiny instant. We both of us wondered whether that lorry was going to plunge down into this gully and crush us to death—you and me. You a young man and me an old woman. In a split, horrible second we both saw ourselves being dashed violently into the concrete-work of this tomb and mingling with the remains of my husband.' She smiled at me with the most disarming geniality conceivable. 'Now, admit it. Didn't you in your fancy hear our groans and shrieks? Didn't you see the driver of that lorry hurtling through the smashed windscreen, a bruised and pulpy mass of flesh and blood and bones? Didn't you envisage the tangle of ruined metal and canes scattered among these tombs and our dying bodies writhing in the midst of it all? Didn't you hear in your fancy our groans and moanings and our anguished gasping screams as perhaps some piece of sharp metal jutted deeper into our entrails? Isn't that what went through your mind in a flash?'

I snapped: 'It's my impression that you possess an extraordinarily morbid outlook, Mrs. Scaife. I might even say diseased.'

She chuckled—innocuously and benevolently. 'Please don't say such things to me, Mr. Woodsley. Remember my age, my boy.'

'Shall we be going back?'

As we ascended to the road, she said that she had often warned Mitchell about this bend. It was an awkward bend. 'I'm always dreading that one day some car or lorry will come hurtling down into the cemetery. I suppose it is a morbid thing to think—but it's perfectly feasible, isn't it?' She glanced at me. 'Isn't it, Mr. Woodsley?'

I made no reply.

We had hardly proceeded fifty yards along the road on our way back when we heard the grass rustling fiercely to the right of us.

It was Bayley, the yard-boy from Eltonsbrody. He came rushing up the incline, and seemed to have emerged from the canefields to the north-west of the depression we had traversed on our way to the cemetery.

Mrs. Scaife halted and frowned. 'What's the matter with the boy?' she murmured. 'What's chasing you, Bayley?' she asked as he came scrambling up to the road. 'Have you seen a ghost?'

He was out of breath.

'Miss Dahlia, Malverne send me to call you home quick, mistress. Soon after you left de house de telephone ring upstairs, Miss Dahlia. Mr. Mitchell call up. He ring up to say dat Master Gregory, he jest dead, mistress!'

5

She nodded and murmured: 'Very well, Bayley. Thank you.'

She did not grow pale. She showed no signs of dismay or sorrow. So unconcernedly did she take the news that both the boy and I stared at her in a wondering silence.

She was staring in the direction of the cemetery with a quiet musing air.

Bayley stammered: 'Miss Dahlia, you—you hear de message; mistress? Master Gregory—he dead. So Mr. Mitchell ring up to say, mistress.'

'Yes. I heard you, Bayley. Master Gregory took ill the day before yesterday with pneumonia. They've been trying everything—all the new drugs. But since last night I knew he would die. Now, run back to the house. Go on. Run off.'

Bayley mumbled something inaudible, gave her a curious glance, then ran off.

I said tentatively: 'Well, I hardly know what to say. By all the codes of politeness, I should be offering you my sympathy—'

'No, no! Please don't,' she interrupted me quickly. 'I understand your feelings, but please refrain from being conventional. I'm not bowed down with sorrow, as you can see, my boy.'

'Oh, I can see that all right.'

'In a way, I am highly delighted—I'm overwhelmed with joy. I can hardly contain myself!' Her voice trailed off into a quavering murmur on the last two words. I noticed one of her hands fumbling at her skirt, and it trembled.

'I know you must think me insane, Mr. Woodsley. But I'm not. I'm an unusual person, that's all. I so wish I could explain—but perhaps if I attempted to it would make matters worse. You'd probably think me even more insane than you do now.' She paced off agitatedly, then halted and looked at me, and there was something appealing in her manner. She clasped her hands together and the look she gave me now contained anxiety as well as supplication. She approached me in two quick paces and said: 'Mr. Woodsley, I do hope you won't leave Eltonsbrody immediately. You'll remain for another week or so, won't you? I do so want someone like you in the house during the next few days. It's going to be a trying time for me, and your presence will help to give me confidence and companionship and—and—oh, will you please stay for another week or two?'

'Well, I'd intended going back to Bridgetown in a day or two. I only planned to spend a week in this part of the island—'

'Please!'

'Very well, very well, Mrs. Scaife. I'll stay on. But I'd be glad to know what's the trouble. Why are you upset? Surely I'm entitled to some kind of explanation—'

'By all means, my boy. You shall have one—but please give me a little time to collect myself. Something important has happened, and I'm unnerved. I must warn you that you may witness some strange little incidents during the next few days, but don't be alarmed. Try to be tolerant—as tolerant as my dear Michael used to be.'

'Would he have understood your being overjoyed at the death of your grandson—your grandson who, you've told me more than once, is the only interest you have in life?'

She glanced at me sharply, as though I had touched on something vital—something she had perhaps imagined I had overlooked. But she betrayed no sign of alarm. She wagged her finger at me. 'Ah! I can see you're trying to trap me into committing myself. Yes, I'm sure Michael would have understood even this. You see, my boy, I'm overwhelmed with a terrible satisfaction and happiness, but I'm also horrified and depressed.' She turned away her face, and her hands kept clenching and unclenching about the folds of her skirt.

On the way back to the house, I listened to her without interruption as she told me in a quiet voice about her grandson, her face grave now, and sorrowful with a sorrow that seemed sincere.

She said that she had seen nothing of Mitchell for about three months before, and more than a year after, his marriage to the Portuguese girl. It was not until Gregory was seven months old that they had met accidentally. He and his Teresa, with the baby, had come down to Bathsheba for a month's holiday, and while taking one of her morning walks, said Mrs. Scaife, she had met them on the main highway not far from St. Aidan's church. She had been quite polite to Teresa—even cordial—but nothing more. She simply could not tolerate Portuguese. Suppose I would scold her for being narrow and prejudiced, but there it was! We all had to have our little oddities. Anyway, she was telling me. Yes, from the instant her eyes had alighted on Gregory that morning she had known that her heart would be lost to him forever. She had made Mitchell promise that he would bring the little fellow to see her often. Mitchell had promised, but he had not kept his word. Took offence, of course, because she had omitted to include Teresa in the invitation. Yes, it must have stung him. However, when

Gregory was about a year old, his grandmother had decided that it was time to take action.

'I had to forget my pride, Mr. Woodsley. The urge to see the dear little fellow was too great. So I phoned Mitchell and asked him if, as a special favour, he wouldn't bring the child to see me. I tried to be as humble as I could, and it worked. He agreed and brought him to see me. It was from then that he and Gregory began to visit Eltonsbrody. I'm always in an ecstasy of fearful joy when Gregory comes. My God! Is it conceivable that I must now use the past tense when referring to that little chap? I bought a camera specially to take his picture every time he came to see me. And that portable gramophone is solely for his entertainment. I have a set of marbles, too, and a rubber ball and a small cricket bat. He and Tappin and I would often play cricket near the kitchen . . .'

Her voice broke. Her eyes were glistening. For a long time she was silent. When she spoke again she might have forgotten my presence.

'Like his grandfather, he had it strong on him. I should have given anything to have watched him die. I should have danced with excitement. To stand beside his bed and watch him slowly strangling with pneumonia—gasping and gradually growing weaker and weaker—Ah! Death! The sweet rapture of death!' She seemed to catch herself. She sighed and said: 'But there! What have I been saying? I've let myself think aloud. Please bear with me, my boy.'

I still refrained from making any comment, studying her, trying to place her, to get her right in my judgment, to make up my mind one way or the other about her. It was difficult, because I had to admit that while her actual words sounded utterly loony, her *manner* was normal. The gleam in her eyes was that of a rational person. It is true that homicidal maniacs are supposed to behave with apparent normality, but nothing could convince me that she had homicidal tendencies. I even tried to tell myself that perhaps she was not so much insane as flighty, but the next moment had to shake my head. There was something too deliberate and reasoned about her air. Every now and then she would give me a twinkling glance that made me wonder whether she were not trying to pull my leg and laughing at me secretly.

When we were entering the driveway of Eltonsbrody she touched my arm and said: 'How much would you like to bet they're standing about in the dining-room discussing me furiously!'

She was right. The servants, except for Malverne, were in the dining-room. We entered the house by way of the kitchen (the front door was kept permanently locked), and we found them in a group near the sideboard, murmuring animatedly. They broke off self-consciously, and Jackman was the first to offer her sympathy.

Her mistress received it as any normal mistress would have done. She thanked her in a quiet voice.

I did not wait to hear more. I went upstairs to get my easel and things, for I intended neither the eccentricities of my hostess nor mysterious events of any kind to prevent me from getting on with my work. It is true I was on holiday, but I am of such a temperament that simply to laze and do nothing for several days in succession—even for one day—means utter misery and boredom. For me to enjoy a holiday I must inter-sperse my lazing with some well-planned bouts of work, or of love-making; either would do as a means to shutting out boredom.

At the top of the stairs, however, I found that the urge to pause and gaze at the two closed doors of the windward rooms proved too strong to resist. Now that Mrs. Scaife had aroused my curiosity in earnest, I was inclined to be suspicious and inquisitive about every little thing.

I moved a few paces along the corridor in an easterly direc-tion, and tried the door of the doctor's old room, deciding that I must satisfy myself that it really was locked.

It did not disappoint me. In fact, the knob seemed stuck tight with dust—or rust—for it would not turn at all.

For a while I stood listening to the wind, I could hear it whistling in under the open eaves (open in tropical fashion for airiness). I could hear it sending whirling draughts circling and writhing within the closed-up space of the room. In my fancy I could see cobwebs hanging in loops and festoons from the old fourposter, and draped all down the old wardrobe that swayed and creaked, and layers of dust on the chest of drawers and wash-stand. I saw myself walking across the room and watching the thick, grey dust rise in a sluggish cloud from the floor round my shoes. I even fancied I could hear the dull, grating crackle of a window as I pushed it up to let the wind come rushing freely in.

Then it occurred to me that there was a key-hole, and why shouldn't I have a peep inside? I shoo-ed off my scruples, bent and applied my eye.

But the blackness of midnight rewarded my inquisitiveness. Some heavy curtain seemed to hang on the inside, or it might be, I told myself, that dust—or rust—and perhaps a little cobweb had blocked the aperture.

I had just begun to wonder if it might be worth my while getting one of my slimmer paint-brushes and doing a little probing with the handle to satisfy myself that it really was dust and cobweb when I thought I heard a sound nearby. A faint, quavering grunt.

I turned and glanced round.

It was Malverne. She was standing in the doorway of her mistress's room, broom in hand, staring mournfully at me.

'Well?' I said. 'What was the grunt for?'

'Oi was sweeping the room,' she said, her face still like a funeral.

'Obviously. I notice you have a broom. Well, go on sweeping.'

She grunted again. Turned off, and before going back into the room, said: 'If you want to see something come in here and Oi will show you.'

Curious at once, I followed her inside, asking: 'What's that? What do you want to show me?'

Her back was to me as I entered, but suddenly she turned round, and her bodice gaped open, revealing her naked breasts.

'What the devil!' I exclaimed, recoiling—then stopped recoiling, shocked but not unpleasantly shocked. 'I see. So this is it?'

Her face unsmiling, still like an undertaker's, she said: 'What you mean by that?'

I replied: 'I mean, your mistress warned me about you. You like to exhibit yourself, she said.'

'How you loike them?' she asked, glancing down sourly at her breasts.

'Very attractive. Excellent pair. And now what's your game?'

She grunted. 'Oi ain' got no game. Oi only want you to look.'

'I am looking—and I'm very entertained, too, believe me,' I told her. 'But remember this, in case you don't know. I'm an artist. It's my living. I've seen dozens of female breasts—and made hundreds of sketches of them. This is nothing new to me.'

'Oi know you does paint pictures and draw. You want to draw me?'

'I can do better than that. I can haul you behind one of the oleander bushes in the front garden and give you what you really want.'

She shrugged her bodice right off, giving me a baleful glance and tossing her head. She grunted, sniffed faintly, too, then said: 'Oi'm not a common girl, you better understand that. Oi don't do no nastiness.'

I chuckled. 'If you ask me, I think you and your mistress are a pair. You're both clean potty.'

'What that mean?' she asked.

'It means you're round the bend. Look, tell me something. Have you ever taken a peep into those two windward rooms, Malverne?'

'What Oi going to peep in them for? Oi can't see nothing through the key-hole loike you been trying to do.'

'Since you've been here, have you never seen the inside of them?'

'Never once. And Oi don't want to.'

'Hasn't your mistress ever asked you to go into them and sweep?'

'Never once. Oi only sweeps in this room and the other room where you staying.' She threw forward her breasts as though for better effect, grunting. Round, erect breasts, faintly blue-veined. Really splendid specimens.

'Now, look, you can put on your bodice again if you like.' I said. 'I've seen enough for the time being. Again let me compliment you—and I really mean it. You have a wonderful figure. Now, tell me about those two rooms. Have none of the other servants gone into them?'

'Only Oi alone the mistress does allow to come upstairs here.'

'Oh. Only you. And why's that? Why can't the others come up?'

'Ask the mistress that. Don't ask me.'

All this while she had not once broken even into the faintest smile. She kept turning herself from side to side in a gentle swaying motion like a mannequin, determined that I shouldn't miss seeing any aspect of her figure. It was incredible, and once I had to blink hard, wondering what sort of creature she could be. She took the cake for abnormality.

'But I'm interested,' I said, trying to suppress the fact that the sight of her figure was beginning to disturb me. 'Why does Mrs. Scaife forbid the rest of them from coming up here?'

She grunted, and said: 'One noight Oi had a dream about the doctor's old room. Oi dream Oi was standing insoide it, and Oi was naked. And the doctor was there looking at me. He look and he look at me, and Oi feel noice. And after he go on looking Oi soigh heavy and tell him Oi'm not that koind of girl. Oi don't do no nastiness.'

I laughed. 'You must have escaped from a mental home, Malverne. Look, I'm not interested in your Freudian dreams. I want to know about those two rooms—'

I was interrupted. The telephone began to ring.

Without hesitation, I moved to the small bedside table and took up the instrument, certain that it must be Mitchell. I said: 'Hallo. This is Eltonsbrody.'

There was a pause—a rather lengthy pause, I thought—then I heard a deep sound that might have been a grunt. The instrument went dead.

I looked round. Malverne had left the room. Puzzled, I was returning the instrument to its cradle when I heard a footstep, and Mrs. Scaife came in. She was smiling. 'So you've answered the phone for me again, my boy. Very kind of you. Was it Mitchell?'

'The person didn't answer,' I said. 'I barely heard a grunt.'

'Ah.'

'But I don't understand it,' I said. 'I thought you told me only Mitchell puts through calls to here.'

'That's so.'

'Well, I'm quite sure it wasn't he who called this time. Whoever it was must have been surprised to hear my voice and just hung up on me.'

'I see.'

'You do? I'm afraid I don't.'

She smiled again. 'Don't let the matter upset you, my boy. He will ring up again. Never fear. You must have given him a scare. That's why he hung up without answering. He expected *me* to answer.'

After a pause, she added: 'He's an old servant. He used to be with us here as a man-of-all-work, but when the doctor died he left and went to Bridgetown to set up in his trade—his favourite trade. He's a maker of tombs.'

'I could have guessed it was something like that,' I said, and at the dryness of my tone she laughed and told me: 'Like myself, he is fascinated by the subject of death. He and

I got on very well together. It was he who built the doctor's tomb.'

'I see.'

'By the way, was Malverne annoying you just before I came in?'

'Far from it. She was entertaining me.'

She uttered deprecatory sounds. 'Well, I warned you, didn't I?'

'Don't let it upset you,' I said, but fidgeted somewhat in embarrassment. 'I'm perfectly capable of handling such situations.'

She sighed. 'When she's dead I'm sure her bosom is going to haunt this house. Just her bosom. It will hover all over the place. She has bared it so often, upstairs here as well as downstairs.'

'I wouldn't mind being haunted by such a ghost,' I murmured, making to leave the room.

She laughed softly. 'Wicked young man! Oh, well! But Michael had a weakness for female bosoms, too. And Borkum.'

'Borkum?'

'Yes. Borkum. The old servant who phoned a few moments ago. He loved female bosoms. He would be entranced by Malverne's idiosyncrasy if he were here.'

'Would he? When last was he here, if you don't mind me asking?'

'I haven't seen him for a long time—nor heard from him. Not since shortly after the doctor's death. But I knew he would get in touch with me to-day. Borkum never fails me.'

As she turned off to go out into the corridor, she added in a low voice: 'He and I have a gruesome little job to perform, Mr. Woodsley.'

'Gruesome?'

'And satisfying. Yes. Gruesome *and* satisfying. For *me* it will be.'

6

Well, I had got accustomed to these horrifying statements, so I expressed no alarm. I merely nodded and murmured: 'Quite so,' and left her.

That morning I spent two satisfying hours before my easel which I set up in a secluded corner of the grounds, in the shade of a mahogany tree—not far from the tool-shed, Tappin's headquarters. I had chosen this spot because from here Eltonsbrody showed up best in the bright morning sunshine, and the trees were arranged and spaced exactly as I wanted them—all save one dwarfed flamboyant which, I decided, would have to be left out, as it obscured an essential patch of red represented by the southern brick wall of the kitchen. To have omitted that bit of red would have upset the harmony of my colour-scheme, and this was unthinkable. Yet, at first, I felt distinctly uneasy about choosing this spot, because I feared that Tappin would have proved a nuisance.

I was wrong. He was curious but most discreet. He strolled up and asked me if I were painting a picture of the house, and when I told him yes, he wagged his head, and said that when he was at school he used to draw, but nowadays he was not so good at it. He used to draw tubs and mugs and chairs, and once he 'did paint a big picture wid water-colours in a choild's animal-book.' Then he showed his discretion by refraining from hanging round to watch me at work. He seemed to sense that I would have found this annoying.

I liked the fellow, and had already had one or two interesting chats with him. Despite his heavy, gauche appearance, he was a man of extremely alert wits, and very intelligent. He read his newspaper carefully, and was well informed about world events. He said he was particularly interested in flying saucers and the Russian Sputnik, and he could tell me all about the doings of Sir Vivian Fuchs and his party in the Antarctic.

As things fell out, Tappin and I had a very serious conversation on Tuesday afternoon (it will be gathered of course, that the events described in the previous pages occurred on Easter Sunday night and Easter Monday morning). How this conversation came about is as follows:

On Tuesday morning, when the servants entered the dining-room for Prayers, Mrs. Scaife, instead of announcing the First Lesson, as customary, told Tappin to go and call McTurk. 'There's something I have to say to all of you this morning, servants,' she went on, 'and I think it best that I say it in the presence of McTurk as well. It concerns him, too.'

Tappin went out and returned in a few minutes with McTurk, a solemn, elderly looking negro. He and Tappin did not get on well together. They were always quarrelling over something, and Tappin (so Jackman told me) went out of his way sometimes to do things 'to mek mock of de old man.'

McTurk came in, a surprised, disgruntled scowl on his wrinkled face. He frowned at his mistress and asked: 'Miss Dahlia, is true you send Tappin to call me in to Prayers?'

'Yes, McTurk, I did.'

Tappin grinned. ''E ain' want to believe me, Miss Dahlia.'

In my easy chair in the sitting-room, I could not suppress a smile.

Mrs. Scaife gave McTurk a quizzical glance. 'You hate being dragged away from your chickens and goats, eh, McTurk?'

McTurk uttered a rumbling sound, and told her, his gaze sulky and lowered: 'It's awroight, Miss Dahlia. Ef you send to call me Oi will come. But Tappin is a man what always meking some joke, and Oi ain' know when to tek him serious.' He took up a position under the picture of Mr. Gladstone, now repaired and in its place again. At once Bayley hissed at him: 'Mr. McTurk, sir, dat picture over you' head was de picture what fall down yesterday morning!'

'What you saying to me, boy?'

Bayley put his hand to his mouth and sniggered—and Jackman became infected, too. Malverne seemed on the point of smiling, then changed her mind and retained her mournful mien. Tappin guffawed, the bloodshot patch in his eye adding to the attractive, roguish twinkle that accompanied his mirth.

Mrs. Scaife looked from one to the other of them and smiled. 'Everyone seems to be in a very good humour this morning.' Her voice was good-natured. She smiled at McTurk and said: 'Don't you take any notice of them, McTurk. Show them you're indifferent to their jibes.'

McTurk uttered more rumbling sounds, sulky and forbidding like a thunder-cloud. There was more tittering from the others, and when it had died down, Mrs. Scaife told them: 'When Prayers are over I want you all to remain for a while until I've said what I have to say. Don't simply go rushing off, please.'

This morning McTurk's deep, rumbling voice gave greater pitch to the murmurous chorus of the Lord's Prayer. But that was the only difference. The wind accompanied them as always with its monotonous drone, and from the poultry-runs and the goat-pens at the back of the house came the same sounds of cackling and clucking and the bleating of the goats.

When the prayer was over, Mrs. Scaife raised her head, looked round and smiled.

'I know you must be curious and a little surprised, but it won't take me long to explain.' She put down the Bible on the sideboard. 'You servants have been with me a number of years, and you've done good service. McTurk, and you, Jackman, you were here since Doctor Scaife's time. And, you, Tappin, came shortly after the doctor's death when Borkum left me to go to Bridgetown to work on his own.' She glanced at Jackman again. 'Jackman, you remember Borkum, don't you?'

'Yes, Miss Dahlia.'

Her mistress nodded. 'Yes, Borkum isn't the kind of man one easily forgets. A splendid man of all trades. Though I must admit, Tappin, that you proved by no means inferior to Borkum in a practical sense. You're not as educated as Borkum, of course. Borkum went to Edinburgh and studied medicine for three years. He could not finish his studies because his father died and his poor mother could not afford to keep him at the university any longer. A great pity, because he has a good brain. He would have made a clever doctor.'

She fell silent, and everybody seemed to be wondering where all this was leading. Suddenly she smiled, looked at McTurk and said: 'You, McTurk, have been extremely efficient. It's true that you seem to have a perpetual grudge against the world, and if we were to judge by your looks and attitude we would have to assume that you hate us all in here with a profound heartiness and would gladly see us dead. Yes, dead!'

McTurk uttered a puzzled sound. The others were frowning puzzledly.

Her manner a little dramatic, though she smiled still in a sort of humorous, sardonic way, Mrs. Scaife continued. 'Wouldn't you,' she said, 'like to see us all dead, McTurk? Wouldn't you like to come into the house late one afternoon when dusk was gathering and find me stretched out on the floor here, stiff and cold and grey—and Malverne, stripped naked to the waist, as she so often likes us to see her, moaning in the corner there, an ugly, gaping wound in her stomach, her bosom slashed across and drenched in blood. Wouldn't you care to see Tappin over there, near that pillar, gasping and groaning and clutching at his throat, dripping blood in thick clots on the floor? And Bayley and Jackman squirming on the rug in the sitting-room, in the grip of some deadly poison? And even our guest, Mr. Woodsley—you might see him in the easy chair where he is now, his head lolling back, his mouth agape in a rigid, fearful grin. Wouldn't such a scene delight you, McTurk?'

Soft exclamations came from them. McTurk, poor fellow, seemed so utterly flabbergasted that he simply stared at her, forgetting, for once, to frown and scowl.

As though unaware of having created a mild sensation,

however, she went on after a smiling pause: 'Yes, I do believe such a sight would do you good, McTurk. Of all my servants, the dark is darkest in you. Further, you have an evil temper, and you're fond of sulking. You bear malice sometimes, though, deep at heart, you're not bad, I know. You're a conscientious worker, and I have a great admiration for conscientious workers. My husband, Doctor Scaife, was like that. Indeed, it was because he was such a conscientious worker that within the last ten years of his life I had to insist on his living here at Eltonsbrody, thirteen miles from the district in which he was practising—for here, at least, no one could call him out at night. It wasn't until he died, of course, that I had a telephone installed here. But I'm straying a little. The temptation to speak of the past—and to dwell upon it in the privacy of my thoughts—has been strong on me these past two or three days. Master Gregory's brief illness and his death have affected me far more than I've betrayed. And apart from this, in many ways that none of you suspect I'm an obsessed woman. . . .'

She broke off. Watching her closely from where I was, I saw her hands fumbling at the folds of her skirt. She left the impression that she had let herself stray into a trance of language. She had said too much, and now she was a little dismayed.

She cleared her throat, and said: 'What I'm really leading up to is this. You McTurk, and you Jackman, you will remember that a day or two after Doctor Scaife died I gave you servants a day's holiday—as a mark of respect to a worthy gentleman.' She glanced quickly from Jackman to McTurk. 'Eh, Jackman? McTurk? You remember this, don't you?'

'Yes, Miss Dahlia,' said Jackman. 'Oi remember.'

'Oi recalls de event,' said McTurk in a formal voice.

'I knew you would. Yes, you couldn't forget.' There was almost a lilt of delight in her voice now. 'It was my way of showing my grief—my simple, unusual way of expressing sorrow. I know very well what this cramped, gossiping little island thinks of me. I've always had the reputation of being an eccentric person—a slightly mad hermit who wouldn't mix with people or have any friends or visitors. Oh, well! I suppose I am queer when looked at with ordinary eyes. But you who have worked with me all these years know me thoroughly— and I think I can say that you have some affection for me. Bayley, you have been here nearly four years. And you, Malverne, four and a half. You were fourteen when you started to work here, weren't you, Malverne?'

Malverne lowered her gaze and nodded. 'Yes, mistress,' she mumbled.

'And, Bayley, you were twelve, weren't you?'

'Yes, Miss Dahlia,' Bayley answered, grinning sheepishly.

'Well, I'm sure we understand each other—and perhaps you won't consider me so queer if I announce that because of Master Gregory's death I've decided to let you have a holiday tomorrow—as a mark of respect to someone I loved dearly.' She seemed to tense slightly as she went on: 'So tomorrow morning you will remain at home. When you go home this evening you won't come out again until Thursday morning.' She glanced from one to the other of them. 'Is that clearly understood?'

There was a murmuring rumble of 'Yes, mistress.'

McTurk fidgeted and said: 'But, Miss Dahlia, who going to feed de Leghorn chickens tomorrow morning ef Oi don't turn up to work? And dose Rhode Island Reds? Dose chickens must get feed or they'll dead by Thursday morning. They are very young chickens.'

'I'll take care of them, McTurk. I'll feed them myself. In fact, I'll take on all the tasks of the household tomorrow. I'll sweep and clean the runs and the goat-pens and feed the fowls and the goats, and I'll prepare my own meals and Mr. Woodsley's. I shall do it as a penance—as a mark of respect to Master Gregory. You needn't be afraid, McTurk. I shall work very hard tomorrow. Years and years ago, as a girl, I knew what it was to sweat, you know. I used to plant canes and potatoes. I've helped my father to catch lobsters and cuttle-fish. I've—'

She broke off, for Malverne had uttered a shriek. She pointed up the stairs. 'Oh, God! Look! Look!'

'What's the matter, Malverne?'

I rose and hurried forward.

The girl began to whimper.

'Malverne, I spoke to you. What is the matter?' Mrs. Scaife's voice was sharp, even a little irritable and alarmed.

'Mistress! Up de stairs! A face look down at me!'

'A what?'

'A face, mistress. A ugly face.'

'What nonsense! Are you dreaming, girl?'

'Mistress, Oi see it. Oi ain' tell no lie.'

I was at the foot of the stairs by now. I looked up, but saw nothing. Behind me, Mrs. Scaife uttered admonitory sounds. 'You're always imagining something, girl. Perhaps you think someone was trying to look down at your bosom. Some man hidden upstairs. But you weren't nude, so why should any man want to look down? And there's no one upstairs, in any case. You know that as well as I do.'

'Mistress, Oi tell you Oi see a face—a ugly face. It look down at me past de banisters. Oi won't tell a lie. As God above me, Oi see it. It glare down at me and turn away quick!'

Without waiting to hear more, I ran up the stairs. At the top I paused and looked about, but the corridor was empty. I went into the old lady's room and peered into every corner, stooped and looked under the bed, opened the door of the small room and glanced in there. No one. Nothing.

I hurried out and went into my room. Nothing in here, either.

The bath and toilet were on the lower storey, so there was nowhere else for me to look. Except in the windward rooms.

I tried spying through the keyholes, but, like the day before, I was disappointed. Darkness greeted my eye at each door.

Outside the doctor's old room, I stood listening—listening to the wind. Monotonously, dolefully, it kept whining and whistling in under the open eaves. Ceaselessly it droned round the house. The wardrobe gave a creak.

My hand, which had been resting on the door-knob, tightened a trifle—and a surprising thing happened. The knob turned.

The door did not open. It was still locked. I pushed it, but it would not yield. But the handle turned easily and without any grittiness.

Yesterday when I had tried it it had been stiff with rust, or dirt, and could not move. But to-day it functioned freely and without the slightest difficulty.

Between yesterday and this morning someone had cleaned and oiled the lock.

7

It was the events of that morning that brought Tappin and me into serious conversation. He approached me at about two o' clock in the afternoon when I was at work under the mahogany tree (I was trying out a new study of Eltonsbrody with the shadows on the eastern side). He asked me if I could spare him a word before the afternoon was out, and I lowered my brush and told him he could go right ahead.

He said: 'Somet'ing on me moind, sir. Oi ain' loike how de mistress behave dis morning. It got me feeling funny.'

'I could have guessed it was that,' I said.

'Miss Dahlia never go on loike how she go on dis morning, sir.' He made a rumbling sound, then asked me in a hesitant voice: 'Sir, you know why she giving us a holiday tomorrow? You t'ink it really because she want to show respect to Master Gregory?'

'I'm afraid I'm no wiser than you, Tappin. Your mistress is an odd bird. I simply can't place her. Sometimes I want to think she's out of her mind—and yet she can seem so confoundedly sane. Oh, by the way, perhaps you can help me with a piece of information. Do you know anything about a chap called Borkum?'

'Borkum? Yes, sir. 'E in Bridgetown now. He does mek tombs. It was he who mek de doctor' tomb.'

'Ah. Of course, of course. The doctor's tomb.'

Tappin told me about the tomb. He said that Miss Dahlia simply worshipped it. Almost every day she went to the cemetery to stand and look at it and smile over it. Every twelfth of January, the anniversary of the doctor's death, she made him go with her and take a large wreath of flowers to put on the tomb. And he always had to be so careful. If he as much as made a thorn scratch the paint she would want to knock his head off. One morning last year she had nearly had a fit because she went and found that a piece of the masonry had been chipped off. Some boy must have thrown a stone and struck the tomb a glancing blow. It was just a tiny flake, but the way his mistress behaved you would have thought a murder had been committed. He had had to get to work right away to repair the damage, and have the tomb repainted. She treated that tomb as though it were a frail child she had to watch over and protect day and night.

I smiled and nodded. 'Most old ladies get sentimental over something or the other, Tappin.'

He shook his head. 'Dat ain' jest sentiment, sir. Dat lady would go stark staring mad ef anyt'ing was to happen to dat tomb.'

'She seems to have been very devoted to her late husband.'

'Oh, lawd! Sir, she can't open her mouth to talk but what she got to say what a foine gentleman de doctor was.' He uttered a groaning sound and shook his head. 'But what Oi can't understand is how she behave over Master Gregory. She always pretend she love dat lil' boy, and now dat he dead she take it so casual. She didn't even go to Bridgetown yesterday for de funeral, sir. Ain't dat what you call funny behaviour, sir?'

'I agree. It did strike me as odd, too. I did mention it to her, but she simply smiled and evaded the subject. I'm afraid I've been officious enough as it is. Remember I'm only a guest here—and a stranger, at that. I can't very well be too insistent in demanding of her explanations for her conduct.'

'Yes, sir, Oi know what you mean. But another t'ing. What you feel cause Malverne to scream out and say she see a ugly face looking down at her from upstairs? You think she really see a face dis morning, sir?'

'What can I say? Personally, I believe Malverne did see something up there, but your mistress wants to make out that the girl was only being imaginative. What I really think is that if we could get a peep into those two closed-up rooms we might learn quite a few things.'

He stared at me, then nodded slowly. He said he was sure I was right. Something very funny had come to Eltonsbrody. In all the years he and the other servants had been working here they had never seen anything like a ghost. And he agreed with me about the two closed-up rooms. He himself had more than once wondered why they should be kept locked up all this time like that. And Miss Dahlia never allowed any of the servants, except Malverne, to go upstairs.

'Yes, Malverne did mention that,' I said. 'Do you know why?'

'It's a rule Miss Dahlia mek, sir. Years and years ago now she mek dat rule. Only Malverne can go upstairs to tidy de rooms. Us other servants must never cross de steps to go upstairs, sir.'

'And has she never given you a reason for this restriction?'

'No, sir. Never. And Oi never worry my head about it, 'cause Oi ain' got no business upstairs. But now you talk, it look funny. Dose two rooms must be hiding somet'ing she don't want us to see.'

'And look here, about Malverne! What sort of creature is she? Has she always had this obsession over her bosom? Why does she behave as she does? It's most unusual.'

He hung his head in some embarrassment, chuckled and said: 'Sir, she not too roight in her head. Oi sure of dat.'

'Has she ever embarrassed you?'

'Oh, lawd! Dat happen so often, sir, Oi accustom to it now. Any toime Oi in de dining-room alone and Miss Dahlia upstairs or out walking, Malverne open her bodice and expose herself. She do it to Bayley, too. And not a smoile on her face, sir. Not a smoile! She mad. You mustn' tek no notice when she behave loike dat.'

'Then you think she could have imagined that face she saw?'

'Well, no, sir. Not dat. She never once say she see anyt'ing queer. Dis de first toime she ever cry out loike she do dis morning. Oi believe she must be did see somet'ing.'

'Where is she now, by the way? I wouldn't mind questioning her on this face she saw.'

'Oi believe she up in Miss Dahlia' room tidying up.' He chuckled. 'Ef you go up now to her she sure to strip and embarrass you.'

'Oh, that doesn't bother me one bit. She has a good figure. Worth seeing. But look here, is this the time she generally tidies up in her mistress's room?'

'Yes, sir—but she was afraid to go up. Oi hear Miss Dahlia not too long ago scolding her and telling her not to be silly, dat nobody or nothing upstairs to harm her.'

'I see. But Malverne still went up?'

'Yes, sir. She didn't want to go, but Oi see her going up.'

'Where is your mistress at this moment?'

'She should be in de garden—de front garden. Dis is de hour she generally go in de front garden to tend de flower-beds. While Malverne tidying up upstairs de mistress always in de front garden.'

'All right. Look here, Tappin, you wait here for me. Don't go. I'll be back in a few minutes.'

'You going to talk to Malverne about de face, sir?'

'Yes. I want a word with her now that her mistress is out of the way. Don't guarantee I'll learn anything more than we already know, but no harm.'

Just to be sure, I went round by the pathway that led to the front garden, and it was as Tappin had said. Mrs. Scaife was busy in the afternoon sunshine. I did not let her see me, and turned off at once and went back round towards the kitchen. I entered by the kitchen door and went upstairs.

As I got to the top of the stairs, I heard a quick, scurrying movement, and Malverne appeared at the door of her mistress's room, a rug in hand. Her face looked startled.

'It's you, sir? Oi hear footsteps on the stairs and Oi wonder—'

'You needn't wonder any longer. It's only me. I want to hear something about this face you saw.'

'De face?'

'Yes, the face you saw from the bottom of the stairs this morning. Can you describe it for me?'

She turned off and made to move back into the room. 'Sir, it was a very ugly face,' she murmured. 'Oi hope Oi never see such a face again.'

'I hope not—but can't you tell me what it was like exactly? Do you think you'd recognise it again if you saw it?'

'Yes, Mr. Woodsley. Oi would.' She sighed and moved right into the room, and I was compelled to follow her. She had dropped the bedroom rug, and I saw what her game was. She was opening up the front of her bodice.

I laughed and said: 'For God's sake, what's the matter with you, girl? Why should you imagine everybody is dying to see you in the raw?'

Solemnly she replied: 'Only men, sir. Oi don't care for women to see me naked.' And she turned with bodice open and breasts bared.

'Look here, you know what I'm beginning to think? You and your mistress must have escaped from a mental home—or a home for tame psychopaths.'

'Oi ain' understand dat word. But Oi not no nasty girl, ef dat what you mean.'

'Very well. Now, about this face. Was it a white man's face?'

'No. It was a black man's face.'

'Oh, good. That's something, anyway. What age would you say he was?'

'You don't loike looking at me?' she said, as though disappointed at my failing to concentrate on her gaping bodice.

'I don't mind at all,' I told her. I clapped my hands in gentle applause. 'I congratulate you on your figure. But there's a time for everything, Malverne. It's mid-afternoon, you know. I don't as a rule show my appreciation of women's breasts at this hour of the day. Now, to go back to this ugly face. How old would you say this black man was?'

'Oi can't say. Oi only see de face quick-quick.'

'What was he doing? Just looking down the stairs?'

'Yes. Jest looking down at me. And he mek a face at me. It frighten me so Oi had to scream out.'

'He grimaced at you? Are you sure?'

'Yes.' She shrugged her bodice right off and stooped and picked up the bedroom rug. I frowned as she moved to the window and began to shake out the rug. 'Why should he have wanted to grimace at you?' I asked. 'Are you sure he really did grimace?'

She nodded, and began to turn herself from side to side like a dress model on parade.

'Look, for God's sake, girl,' I told her, 'you're giving me the jitters. I'm not accustomed to being sexually stimulated at this time of day. I mean it. Put on your bodice and let's talk about what you saw this morning. I can meet you this evening if you like.'

She gave me a scandalised stare. 'Oi don't do no nastiness with men,' she said. 'Oi is not dat koind of girl, Mr. Woodsley.'

'All right. I give up. I'm going—'

'Please don't go till Oi finish tidying up in here, sir. Oi 'fraid.'

'What are you afraid of?'

'What Oi see dis morning, sir. It was a bad face. It froighten me.'

'Didn't it seem like the face of a solid human being? It didn't seem shadowy, did it? I mean like a ghost?'

'No. It was a real face, sir. A black man. But ghoses does look real. My aunt and uncle say they see plenty ghoses.'

'They live down at Martin's Bay, don't they?'

'Yes. Oi is an orphan. My fadder and mudder dead. My aunt and uncle does see their ghoses plenty toimes.'

'But you're sure this face this morning wasn't a ghost? It looked like a black man's face? A real black man?'

'It moighta been a ghost. Oi ain' know.' She began to sway herself from side to side, waggling her breasts seductively.

I sighed, gave her a pat on the shoulder and went out, despite her appeal to me to stay. Half-way down the stairs, I glanced back and saw her gazing down at me, her face mournful and still appealing (I was to recall it with much remorse sooner than I had thought. Even as I went down I was feeling a bit callous for leaving her up there alone; already a bit remorseful, in fact).

I went out back to where my easel stood. Tappin was there awaiting me. He gave me a look of inquiry, and I smiled and told him: 'Just as you predicted. She didn't waste any time to shed her bodice. But at least, I managed to get this out of her. It was the face of a black man—and she seems to think it was a solid face. Not that she doesn't believe it might have been a ghost—'

'She not too roight in her head, sir. You can't go too much by what she say—but Oi believe she see somet'ing dat froighten her dis morning.' He chuckled and pointed towards the house. 'Look, sir. She at de window shaking out de rug. Naked as she born.'

I looked and saw Malverne at the window of her mistress's room. She still had not put on her bodice yet.

'Nutting strange, sir,' said Tappin. 'More dan once she do dat when me or Bayley in de yard here working. Purposely stand naked before de window and call out to me.'

'Wait. Look! Look, Tappin!'

I caught the man's arm and gasped. He followed my gaze, and we saw that Malverne had turned off from the window, the rug still in hand. She recoiled, as we watched—then darted out of sight with a scream.

'What the devil!'

Without hesitation, Tappin and I began to hurry towards the house.

'Somet'ing must be froighten her again,' said Tappin.

A vague thudding sound came from in the house accompanied by another scream from Malverne. Then we heard another scream—Jackman's.

'Oh, God, oh, God, oh, God!' Jackman screamed.

Out of the corner of my eye I saw Mrs. Scaife appear round the corner of the building, a garden-trowel in hand.

Jackman nearly collided with Tappin and myself as we tried to rush in through the kitchen door both together. She was grey with fright and panic. She wrung her hands and gasped: 'Oh, God, Mr. Woodsley sir! Come quick! Malverne fall down de stairs. She look as ef she dead.'

8

We found her half-nude, as I had left her not many minutes before. She had dropped the rug at the top of the stairs. It must have tripped her up. She was moaning and turning from side to side, but was unconscious.

Mrs. Scaife asked me to take her upstairs to her bedroom. She helped me, and we took her up as carefully as we could and put her into the big fourposter. Mrs. Scaife drew a blanket over her nudity, and got on the telephone. 'I must ask Doctor Dayton to come,' she said. 'He's in Bridgetown, but he'll come. He always liked Michael.'

An hour later Doctor Dayton arrived, and he said it was rather serious. She had sustained severe injuries to her head and her spine, and was suffering from partial paralysis and concussion. When I asked him he said that it was quite feasible that a fall down the steps could have been responsible for the injuries. He and I were alone in the dining-room just before he left when I put the question to him. He looked surprised and asked me if I had any particular reason for asking the question.

I shrugged and said: 'No, no. I just wondered. As a boy, I've fallen down stairs umpteen times without any serious results.'

He smiled and said: 'Well, of course, what doesn't happen in a year can happen in a split second. I remember a case like it two years ago in Bridgetown. Those stairs are very steep. She must have fallen head foremost. This bedroom rug, it's obvious, must have tripped her up. You saw her with it at the window, you said, when she screamed and turned off?'

'Yes, yes. I did see her with the rug.'

'Anyway, her mistress is being very decent about it. She has agreed to have a nurse come here and take care of her.'

'She has, has she?'

He nodded. He was a short, thick-set man, forty-ish and with slightly projecting teeth. A good-humoured fellow, and I had taken to him on the spot. 'Yes. She's a good sort, Mrs. Scaife—if a little peculiar in her ways. And a nurse is absolutely necessary. To try to remove her to the hospital thirteen miles away would be as good as killing her off right away. She couldn't stand the trip. Must be kept very, very quiet.'

'An operation wouldn't be of any use?'

'Her heart is too weak. She suffered from chronic dyspepsia, Mrs. Scaife says, and I can well believe it. Very shaky heart.'

After he had taken his departure, I paced for a long time in the sitting-room, thinking things over. Why, I asked myself, had she uttered that scream? What had frightened her? Mrs. Scaife had tried to assure the doctor that the scream was nothing to be taken seriously. 'A most hare-brained girl, doctor. She must have imagined she heard some strange noise that was frightening. Perhaps the wind in one of the closed up rooms. There's an old wardrobe that creaks in Michael's room.' I had said nothing, but I had known that she was trying to put the doctor off the scent.

I felt convinced that it was no mere 'strange noise' that had scared Malverne. The girl had *seen* something again that had made her scream as she had and dash for the stairs. Could it have been the same face that had frightened her that very morning?

Hearing footsteps on the stairs, I glanced round and saw Mrs. Scaife coming down. She joined me in the sitting-room. Her face was flushed, and her eyes gleamed with excitement. A wisp of her hair hung loose down her forehead. 'Oh, Mr. Woodsley, isn't it terrible? Just terrible? The poor girl! The doctor says there's very little hope for her.'

'He didn't put it quite like that to me—but he did say it's rather serious.'

'Yes—very serious.' She sighed softly. 'I'm horribly depressed—yet I'm overjoyed, too.'

'You are, are you?' I gave an expressive grunt. But she ignored its implication and said: 'I came down to tell you not to be troubled over the matter of accommodation. We'll make out somehow, I'm sure. You can still keep your room.'

'But haven't you given your room over to Malverne?'

'Yes. So I have. And I'm having a small cot erected for the nurse. It used to be kept stored in the junk-room near the pantry. I never thought we should need it some day. But don't upset yourself, my boy. I'll make out, no fear. I don't mind being inconvenienced sometimes—especially at such a time as this. You should see the shadow . . . oh! I'm sorry.'

'What? What were you going to say about a shadow?'

'Nothing, nothing. I was allowing myself to think aloud. Silly habit of mine at times, my boy. Take no notice of me. I'm so overwhelmed. So keyed up.' She sighed again, and squeezed her hands together ecstatically. 'Tappin is upstairs now seeing after the cot for me. He's such a useful fellow—'

'Tappin upstairs? But—'

'Yes. He's in my room fitting up the cot. I told him to be as quiet as he could. The doctor said Malverne must not be disturbed—'

'But I understood that Malverne was the only servant you allowed to go upstairs.'

She gave me a sharp glance. 'Ah. What's this? Who told you

that? Yes, it is a strict rule of mine—but I had to break it to-day because of force of circumstances.'

'And would it be too inquisitive of me to inquire why you made such a rule?'

She held up her hand. 'Never use the word "inquisitive" to me. You must consider it your right to ask me anything you like.' She gave me a teasing glance and added: 'Not, of course, that you must always expect to get satisfactory answers to every question you ask. Oh, by the way, you did know that a nurse is coming, didn't you? Did the doctor mention it?'

'He did—but why have you changed the subject so abruptly?'

Ignoring me, she prattled on: 'I really want to do my best for Malverne. She's an orphan. Only an old invalid aunt and an uncle alive. The MacMullochs once had her on their plantation—they adopted her unofficially—but when her uncle and aunt heard rumours of the unusual ways of the MacMullochs they took her away from them. A pity. The MacMullochs are a good family. They help the peasants a lot. I must remember to tell Tappin to take a message to Malverne's aunt and uncle this evening on his way home. I've had to cancel the holiday I promised the servants tomorrow. It's most annoying, because I really wanted to get them all out of the way for at least twenty-four hours.'

She kept fidgeting in her garrulity, and under her buoyancy I detected something feverish and unnatural. Yet the gay, light note in her voice seemed to ring true. She baffled me completely.

It was nearly five o'clock, and the weather appeared to be undergoing a change. Clouds had massed in the sky, slate-grey and thundery. The wind, however, was still as strong as ever, and the air could not be described as oppressive. Now and then a fine drizzle would throw a thick, misty curtain round the house, blurring the vista so that the cottages down at Bathsheba and Martin's Bay looked flimsy and unreal like cottages in a water-colour sketch.

The sitting-room was gloomed and bleak, alive with shifty, uncomfortable draughts, and the dark walls and the heavy Victorian furniture in no way decreased the general cheerlessness.

'I do wish it would rain,' Mrs. Scaife remarked, glancing outside. 'My celery is badly in need of a good sousing. I don't know what would have happened to the poor things by now if I hadn't been watering them twice a day.' She turned off abruptly and said she had better be going upstairs to see how Tappin was getting on.

I resumed my pacing—and my pondering of the situation.

I cursed myself for not having remained upstairs with the girl until she had finished her cleaning activities. Especially as she had asked me to. What, I asked myself, could possibly have appeared on the scene to scare her into screaming? Had someone entered the room? The owner of the ugly face she had seen from the foot of the stairs that morning?

I remembered the old servant, Borkum. Could there be any connection between that telephone call and the face Malverne said she saw? Again, there was that cleaned and oiled door lock. Who had cleaned it? I had tried the knob of the other door after lunch, and found that it worked freely, too. Had anybody gone into those two windward rooms within the past twenty-four hours? If so, for what purpose? Suppose Borkum had been concealed in one of the rooms, and had emerged briefly and seen Malverne half-nude in her mistress's room? Mrs. Scaife had said that he was fond of females' bosoms. Could he have tried to attack the girl? But what, in the first place, would he want to be concealed in the house here for?

At this point, my conjecturings came to an end. Above the howling of the wind I heard the voice of my hostess. It came from upstairs, and it was shrill with anger and alarm.

I dashed for the stairs. Took the steps three at a time. As I got to the top, I heard Mrs. Scaife's voice again.

'Come, Tappin! Speak up! Tell me! What were you doing outside that door?'

A few yards further along the corridor, I made out the big, awkward form of Tappin. He was staring at his mistress in a silly, baffled manner.

'Tappin! I'm speaking to you! Answer me! When you left my room a few minutes ago I assumed that you would have gone downstairs at once. Why didn't you? Why did you stop to make a peering investigation through that keyhole? What could have possessed you to do such a thing, Tappin? Tell me. Come on. This is serious, I'm waiting.' There was a cracked note in her voice.

Tappin lowered his head and began to mumble something.

'What's that? What's that? I haven't heard. Repeat it.'

'Mistress, Oi didn't do it for no reason.'

'You didn't do it for any reason?' Her voice was a shriek. 'Don't tell me that! Don't dare tell me that! That's a lie! You know it's a lie! You must have had a reason. What was it? What did you expect to see in there? That is my old bedroom. It has been locked up for years and years—like the doctor's next to it. What did you hope to see in it that would interest you? Come, loosen your tongue! This is important. I want to know what was your motive. I'm determined to find out.'

Tappin said nothing.

Mrs. Scaife moved up the corridor a little closer to him.

'Tappin, I'm speaking to you. Are you going to tell me? Come. I'm very serious.' Of a sudden her voice became coaxing. 'Tell me, Tappin man. Come. What was it you expected to find in that room? I'm really curious to know. I *want* to know. Did anybody tell you I had something strange concealed in there?'

The man shook his head and mumbled: 'Miss Dahlia, Oi ain' had no definite reason, mistress.'

She stared at him, tense. I could see that this time she was genuinely shaken. Tappin's curiosity had driven fear deep into her. But fear of what?

She sighed and said: 'So you won't tell me. Or perhaps it may be that you really have nothing to tell. It was sheer inquis-

itiveness that made you do it. The ugly face Malverne fancied
she saw up here this morning.' She spoke as though to reassure
herself, as though hoping she would see him give some sign
indicating confirmation that her surmise was correct.

But Tappin kept his head bent, dejected, ashamed.

Mrs. Scaife smiled and said: 'Very good. We'll have to have
this matter straightened out at once. Stand just where you are.
Don't go.'

She turned, and as though unaware of my presence only a
yard or two behind her and of the faces of the three servants
at the foot of the stairs, took two quick paces into her room.

Round the house the wind howled in a monotonous,
mournful passion of sound, and downstairs in the sitting-
room the windows kept rattling off and on.

Mrs. Scaife appeared from her room. She carried a bunch
of keys.

'Come, Tappin. Follow me!' She spoke calmly, and Tappin
began to follow her reluctantly along the corridor.

She glanced back. 'Mr. Woodsley! You, too, please! Come. I
want you both to accompany me.'

'What's the matter? What do you want with me?'

She stopped at the door of her old room. 'We're going to
settle the mystery, Mr. Woodsley. That's what I want with you.
I want to show you the grisly objects Tappin was hoping to see
when he peered through the keyhole here a few moments ago.
Come. We'll all go in and look round.'

She inserted the key into the lock.

9

As she pushed the door open a dry, musty smell of rotting
clothes and wood and paper struck our senses—and another
smell was too vague for me to identify at once, though it gave
me a bit of uneasiness.

A huge fourposter bed loomed before us in the rainy light

that filtered in through the dirt and salty encrustations on the window panes. It was faultlessly made up with sheet and counterpane and pillows with embroidered cases, the tester overhead hung around with a heavy lace frill. But this bed must have been made up many years before, for the counterpane and pillows were covered with a thick layer of grey dust, and the tester billowed down as though weighted with wood-rot and a dense wealth of dust. The lace frill was yellow and blotched. Pillows, sheets, tester, lace frill and bedposts were all linked together in a dim, involved network of cobwebs.

Two or three feet away, on one side of the bed, stood a tall, white cupboard, and on the other side, with a much wider separating space, a mahogany chest of drawers, both thickly coated with dust and draped with cobwebs. Just beneath one of the two western windows, and in the space between the chest of drawers and a marble-topped washstand, stood an old-fashioned, flat-topped travelling trunk, this, however, unlike the washstand and the chest of drawers, bearing hardly any dust or cobwebs.

Mrs. Scaife turned and pointed at the door. 'Look, Tappin! See! It's this curtain behind the door that prevented you from seeing into the room when you spied through the keyhole. It used to act as a protection for the few garments I hung behind the door on pegs. There is no mystery in it. It hangs over the keyhole just by accident. I didn't block the keyhole to prevent spies from looking into the room.'

She jerked her thumb. 'The other room over there—the doctor's room—is the same. There is a curtain behind the door that prevents inquisitive persons like yourself from looking through the keyhole into the room—but, as in here, it's simply an accidental circumstance.' She pointed at the bed. 'Look! My old bed! It's decorated with cobwebs. But there's nothing else very remarkable about it that I can see. And you're at liberty to look under it. You'll see nothing startling.' She beckoned to him. 'Go on. Stoop down and look. Satisfy yourself.'

Tappin made no attempt to stoop down.

'Go on! I insist. Stoop down and look. Make sure there's no fearful monster with green eyes and a slobbering mouth crouched up under the bed.'

Just as the man was stooping to look under the bed, something struck me with a wallop. There was not a speck of dust on the floor!

I glanced sharply about me. Under the washstand there was dust and cobwebs, and when I bent to follow Tappin's example and looked under the bed I saw dust and cobwebs there, too. Which meant—and it was the only conclusion I could come to—that this room had been swept out very recently: at least, the walking space of the floor had been swept; the section between the door and the bed and the section between the bed and the chest of drawers.

I took a pace past the foot of the bed, and glanced down at the two or three feet of floor space between the tall cupboard and the bed. There was dust—thick dust.

While Mrs. Scaife was ranting at Tappin and pulling open drawers to show him that nothing suspicious or horrible or monstrous (the adjectives were her own) was concealed in them I took the opportunity to examine the floor more closely.

The light was fading rapidly, but my eyes are very good. The section between the door and the bed revealed nothing very interesting, but when I came to the space between the bed and the chest of drawers I found myself frowning and nodding to myself. I felt like Sherlock Holmes pouncing upon a new clue and gloating quietly.

Out of the greyness of the floor there emerged an oblong patch that looked unusually clean—and around this patch I could make out distinctly one or two dim stains, brownish or bluish. The general impression was that a piece of linoleum or oil-cloth of oblong shape had been spread out here and that dirty water or some darkish liquid had run off it and left the stains so that when the linoleum had been removed this rectangular patch had remained. The stains looked fresh, too, and I decided to myself that whatever had happened to cause their presence had happened within the past twenty-four hours.

I wrinkled my nose, trying to place that smell I had detected on first entering. A sickly, sweetish smell. Stale perfume? No, not perfume. Ammonia? Perhaps—and yet . . . No, not ammonia. Nothing sharp or volatile about it. I wanted to tell myself that it must be the odour of putrefaction, that some corpse had lain in this room not many hours before, but I rejected the idea as too sensational and fantastic.

I didn't have much time to dwell on the matter, for Mrs. Scaife turned upon me (I nearly said pounced) and asked me if I, too, would like to have a look into the drawers. 'Perhaps you might be able to convince this prying idiot that I keep no grisly relics in here, Mr. Woodsley. Come, have a look, please, my boy.'

I declined the offer.

'Well, then, the cupboard, perhaps!' she cried, and crossing to the tall white cupboard, wrenched it open. The door came away with a crackle of wood-rot and a swish of cobweb. A musty blast rained through our senses, and dust reached out in grey, swirling tentacles. I coughed and stepped back a pace, but my hostess, unaffected, waved her hand dramatically and shrilled: 'See! Old clothes! All rotting. Skirts and bodices and a few items of underwear. Left in here as a monument to a happy married life. Yes, that is why this room was locked up, Tappin. Because when the doctor died I knew that my life was over and that henceforth I should exist only in a cloud of memory. My happiness, and my real life—the life that was full and rich—was locked away into these two rooms after the doctor died. I had meant never to open them again. I had meant never to set eyes upon anything in these two rooms, but merely to pass outside in that corridor and smile in quiet memory at all that lay stored in here. But now! This evening, because of your stupid prying, Tappin, I have had to break my resolve. I had to unlock this door and come in here to satisfy you that nothing grim is concealed within these walls.'

I gave a laugh, and, in my usual tactless way, broke out: 'Are you trying to make out that this room has not been entered since you locked it up after your husband's death in 1950?'

She jerked her head round and stared at me. 'What do you mean, Mr. Woodsley? Why do you ask that?'

'Because I have good reason to believe that someone was in here within the past twenty-four hours.'

'In here?'

'Yes, in here, Mrs. Scaife—and in the next room, too.'

'Are you mad? Are you—but—but I never heard anything more absurd! My God! My God!' She turned off, and instinctively I put out my hand, for she tottered as though about to faint.

But she recovered. She beckoned weakly towards the door, and Tappin and I went out. Without a word, she followed us, shut and locked the door and went hurrying along the corridor. She disappeared into her room, and I was sure I heard a sound that resembled a sob.

Tappin accompanied me downstairs, a gloomy, half-fearful look on his face. In the dining-room, Jackman and McTurk and Bayley stood in a group near the sideboard murmuring. They turned and looked at us with wondering, frightened eyes. Then Jackman said: 'Mr. Woodsley, sir, what happening upstairs? What wrong wid de mistress, sir?'

'Your question voices my own thoughts, Jackman,' I replied. I lit a cigarette, and offered one to McTurk, but he refused. 'Oi never smoke dose t'ings, sir,' he smiled gloomily. 'Only a poipe.'

Padding footsteps sounded in the pantry, and Walter and Patrick entered.

McTurk turned with a growling scowl on Bayley. 'But boy, why you loose dese dogs? Ent Oi tell you not to loose dem?'

Bayley looked dismayed. 'McTurk, Oi forget. They always loose every afternoon, and Oi forget you tell me not to loose dem.'

'Awright—well, you jest go now and chain dem up again. You too forgetful for a young boy.'

As Bayley called to the dogs I asked McTurk: 'Why can't they be released this afternoon?'

He shrugged and replied: 'Sir, Miss Dahlia told me dat Oi must see and keep dem chain up till she tell me to loose dem. All last noight they had to remain chain up near de kennel, sir-and all to-day. Oi feel sorry for de poor animals, sir, but de mistress order me to do it.'

'When did she give you these orders?'

'Last noight before Oi go home, sir. She come to de goat-pen and say Oi must see and not loose de dogs till she tell me. She ent give me no reason, sir.'

'She tell me de same, too, sir,' said Tappin who seemed to have regained his self-possession now. 'She tell me not on any account to unchain de dogs till she tell me.'

'I see.'

'Dis de first toime she ever give such orders,' McTurk rumbled. He shook his head. 'Somet'ing gone wrong wid dat ole lady, sir.'

Suddenly Mrs. Scaife's voice screamed down from the top of the stairs.

'Tappin! Bayley! McTurk!'

Tappin started. McTurk raised his head sharply. Bayley grunted. Jackman exclaimed softly.

Mrs. Scaife came down half-way, and said: 'What are those two dogs doing in the house? McTurk, Tappin! Didn't I give strict orders that they were not to be released until I gave the word?' Her voice was harsh. In the dusk she had a stiff, forbidding, imperious look, standing there on the stairs.

McTurk rumbled out an explanation.

'Very well,' she said coldly. 'See that you don't suffer any more lapses of memory, Bayley. Take them outside and chain them up again, and then come back. I have something for you to do.'

'Yes, mistress.' The boy hurried out with the two dogs.

'Tappin, I want you to go into the junk-room and get out that old deck-chair. Have it dusted and then bring it upstairs.

I want it put into my old room. I'm going to occupy my old room temporarily.'

'Awright, Miss Dahlia,' said Tappin, and went off towards the pantry.

'And, McTurk, I want you to clean the old table-lamp thoroughly for me. You'll find it in the junk-room, too. When you have cleaned it, have it filled with oil and leave it on the dining-table.'

'Very well, Miss Dahlia.' McTurk moved off, his old-man face very perplexed. I saw his lips moving silently.

'Jackman, what of my dinner? It's nearly six o' clock.'

'Yes, mistress. It nearly ready. De water boiling now to make de tea, mistress.'

'Well, please go back to the kitchen and brew the tea.'

I was about to move into the sitting-room when she called down to me: 'Oh, Mr. Woodsley, I'm sorry to bother you, but would you mind lighting the lamp for me on the dining-table?'

'Not at all.'

Bayley came out at this point, and Mrs. Scaife told him that she wanted him to run out for her. 'Go down to the shop at Bathsheba and buy me three candles.' She held out a coin, and the boy went up and took it from her, then hurried down the stairs and out of the room. His mistress turned and went upstairs, seeming to melt into the gloom at the top of the stairway.

It was virtually night now, and after I had lit the lamp on the dining-table the weak, yellowish light, if anything, seemed to deepen the shadows in corners and niches all over the room. The long, dark mahogany dining-table gleamed mysteriously, and the glassware on the sideboard reflected the lamplight in a soft array of distorted ruddy eyes squinting from the sides of tumblers and decanters and flagons and sugar-bowls. In the midst of them, dim and dusty-grey, the clump of brain coral lay with a crouching air as though in waiting for some uncertain and sombre event.

The wind kept whistling and moaning round the house.

I could sense it pushing and driving against the beams and boards and the stone that went to make up the structure. I could sense it trying to pierce its way into the rooms past the crevices of the windows. And the groping whimsical draughts. Even as I stood there in the dining-room I could feel one of them curling round my ankles as though it were an invisible serpent emerged from the dense gloom under the long table.

I went into the sitting-room and looked out at the weather. The sky had cleared up considerably. Only one or two slate-grey rags moved in it now, heading for Hackleton's Cliff which frowned menacingly in the southwest.

Down in Martin's Bay, one or two yellow lights gleamed in the deep mist of darkness that had settled upon the cottages and rocks. Unlike at Bathsheba, there were no electric lights down there. Only lamplight. Lamplight in tiny cottages made of wood and unpainted shingles in which farmers and fisher-folk lived. Down there, too, I remembered, was the Well Pit, the bottomless crevasse over which the sea boiled day and night and into which boats were sometimes sucked down never to be seen again.

The uneasiness in me had increased threefold, and I think that but for the knowledge that the nurse was coming—for, of course, her coming meant welcome companionship for me and someone rational, I hoped, in whom I would be able to confide all that was happening in the house—but for this fact I think I would have broken my resolve and gone back to Bridgetown the following morning, leaving Eltonsbrody and its mysteries to take care of themselves.

This sitting-room gave me the gooseflesh. There was that epergne, for instance, on the centre table which, in this uncertain light, had a most disturbing effect upon me. Intricately wrought out of pale-green glass, thin, opaque and convuluted around the top, it kept persistently obtruding its presence upon my gaze. I seemed unable to avoid it. It was forever sidling itself into the corner of my eye, elegant and spectral, hovering there above the heavy round-topped table as though determined to mock me with its glassy elusiveness. At length, it got on my nerves so much that I left the room, deciding to go upstairs and do a little reading.

I was half-way up the stairs when something made me pause.

The floor of the upper storey was on a level with my chin, and I was just about abreast of the door of the doctor's old room on my right, across the corridor. Standing where I was, I was aware of a strong, dank smell. At first, I thought it was another instance of my fancy getting the better of me, so I retreated two or three steps down. The smell thinned off at once. Descending right to the bottom, I found that I could discern no smell at all. Then I went up again. The smell struck me again—strong, unmistakable. Dank and earthy. I might have been standing on the brink of a freshly opened grave. I turned my head and looked at the silent blankness of the door on my right, and knew without any doubt that it was out of the doctor's old room that this deathly odour was seeping.

10

I found that I could not read, so I smoked and stood at one of the two western windows in my room watching the sunset tints over Hackleton's Cliff. Small clumps of alto-cumulus from a bright pink merged into gamboge, and then into a dull sienna, edged with bluish white, then the sienna gave way to a slate-grey, sombre and peaceful. Some of the higher clouds dissolved into the lapis-lazulis of the sky, and the lone coco-nut palm on Hackleton's Cliff suddenly stood out jet-black and significant: a plumed sentry watching over the rugged landscape. The chill of night tingled on my cheeks, and the air smelt of the sea—iodine-tinged and fishy. I could hear the peep-peep of the chickens in the coops, and the monotonous hissing rustle of the casuarinas which, as usual, looked unreal and not of the earth. Their needle-like foliage kept fingering delicately against the sky, phantom-wise and indefinite. They might not have been trees at all but mere segments of the deep twilight congealed into wisps of greater density: shapeless shadow-nuclei out of which the night would grow and send out tentacles to envelop the rocks and the canefields and the tiny shingled cottages and the sea visible now as a dull purple haze encircling the jagged coastline.

Overhead, the sky was clear with a look of frosted glass. The thundery clouds of the afternoon had vanished, and one or two stars were winking, blue-white and inscrutable, chilly, too, like the feel of the rain-cooled air.

After a while, I became aware of sounds in the corridor, and assumed that it must be Tappin bringing up the deck-chair for his mistress. She was going to occupy her old room temporarily, she had said. Her intention, no doubt, was to sleep in the deck-chair. Perhaps tomorrow she would have the big four-poster dusted and prepared for use.

I kept remembering the clean patch, oblong-shaped, on the floor of the room she was going into. And the stains around the edges. What had happened in there last night? And the odour of the grave coming from the doctor's room—and the sweetish smell in the other windward room—what conclusions could anyone come to about these things?

Then there was the travelling trunk. She had not opened that. Why? She had taken pains to reveal to Tappin the contents of the chest of drawers, and had pulled open the door of the cupboard and dramatically pointed at the old clothes hanging in it. But why had she chosen to overlook the trunk? Was there something ghastly locked up in that trunk?

A car was turning into the driveway. It must be the nurse.

I made my way downstairs, Mrs. Scaife close behind me. As I was about to enter the sitting-room she called to me: 'Very nice of you to come down to help me greet the nurse, Mr. Woodsley!' She spoke in her old affable, benevolent manner, and seemed to have completely forgotten the scene she had created upstairs only a short while before. Lamp in hand, she accompanied me to the front door.

'I do so like to meet people for the first time, my boy,' she said—and there was a genuine ring of pleasurable anticipation in her voice. 'One never can tell what one may not see on their faces,' she added softly.

The nurse turned out to be a much younger person than I had expected. She looked no more than twenty-three, and was attractive, too. No stiff, gaunt, hawk-faced creature, practical and efficient and bossy, as I had pessimistically envisaged. Her name was Linton—Grace Linton, though it was not until the following day that I discovered her first name. She had blue-green eyes, and I noted in them a pleasant, half-humorous glint that instantly appealed to me.

'I'm Miss Linton,' she said to Mrs. Scaife. 'I think you're expecting me.'

'Yes, yes. Of course.' To my surprise. Mrs. Scaife's voice was curt, almost insulting in its complete lack of cordiality. I saw her face in the light from the lamp, and was struck by the scowl which had taken the place of her smile. Her face looked positively hostile. She turned abruptly to me and said: 'Mr. Woodsley, would you be so good as to show Miss Linton upstairs to my room?' Before I could even open my mouth to reply she jerked round and said to the nurse: 'You'll find the patient in much the same condition in which Doctor Dayton left her, Miss Linton. The cot is for your own use—and dinner will be served for yourself and Mr. Woodsley at seven.'

And she went off. She made her way towards the dining-room and vanished into the pantry.

Miss Linton looked at me. 'Is there anything the matter? Isn't she keen on having me here?'

'So keen that she went to the trouble of having the cot she mentioned erected for you, and she's been making all sorts of fussy preparations for your arrival. But don't let her upset you.' I touched my temple. 'I don't believe all is right up here. Round the bend, that's my diagnosis. Shall we go up?'

The earthy odour had disappeared, and I decided that, for to-night, at least, I would tell her nothing about the frighteningly puzzling business of the past two days. I didn't want to get her scared.

A little later when we were dining, I asked her what she thought about the patient. 'Any signs yet of returning consciousness?'

'Not yet,' she said.

We ate in silence for an interval. The wind moaned and whooped round the house, tirelessly, and once or twice came the flap-flap of the canvas sacking in the pantry.

Surreptitiously I kept watching Miss Linton's profile, deciding that it was quite a nice profile. She had poise, and her starched, white nurse's uniform looked well on her. Very good figure, too. Not up to Malverne's standard, perhaps, but extremely presentable.

Once she shivered and remarked on the draughtiness of the room, and I nodded and said: 'Never came across a place for draughts like this. They come crawling along the floor. They swoop down your back from the ceiling. They shoot out of corners. And listen to the wind!'

'Yes, it's very strong.' She gazed round slowly, as though taking note of the place for the first time. Could it be my imagination or was there already a look of uneasiness in her eyes? 'It seems to be a very old house. The furniture is so old-fashioned.'

I grunted assent. 'Didn't you notice the date over the front door? No, but, of course, it was too dark for you to see it. It was built in 1887.'

Another silence fell between us.

The windows in the sitting-room prattled in a sudden onslaught from the wind, and I felt a draught twining its way, chilly and tickling, up my leg. Though the windows were closed, intangible gusts of air seemed to rush in full anguished fury across the dim spaciousness of the sitting-room, melting mysteriously just as they were on the point of assaulting us here at this long, dark table. Now and then the flame of the lamp would shudder and reach abruptly for the top of the glass shade that imprisoned it, as though at the beckoning of some invisible finger, then as abruptly subside and grow steady again, red and unconcerned, spilling its soft light upon everything round it with a quiet, almost slyly intelligent passivity.

More than once I found my gaze straying towards the clump of brain-coral on the sideboard. Like the epergne in the sitting-room, it was one of the objects in this house to which I had taken a dislike. The epergne possessed a disturbing elusiveness in the semi-dark, and the brain-coral seemed to me sly and secretive as though it knew much that I would like to know, and deliberately mocked at my ignorance.

To keep from seeing it I tried again to concentrate on Miss Linton's profile, and was engaged in this occupation when I noticed her brows lower slightly. She had been looking idly towards the stairway, the bottom half of which was coated dimly with the light from the lamp. The higher steps were in gloom—a gloom that preceded the utter blackness that prevailed in the corridor upstairs.

I said: 'You seem to be contemplating those stairs very earnestly. As if you might be weighing the possibility of a headlong fall down them.'

She laughed. 'Nothing so alarming. Did you drop anything on the steps when you were coming down?'

'Drop anything? Anything like what?'

'Look there,' she said. I followed her gaze. 'I saw it since we first sat down to eat, but I didn't think of remarking on it. It looks like a skein of thread—or is it some kind of watch-guard?'

I saw it, too. I had not noticed it before. A dark object coiled in a semi-circular loop. It was lying on the third step from the bottom.

I rose and crossed to the stairway, bent and had a closer look. My hand reached out to pick it up. Then I hesitated.

'What's it?' she asked.

'Come and see.'

She rose at once and joined me.

'Why, it's a lock of hair!' She stretched out and picked it up. Then a look of repugnance came to her face, and she tossed it down. 'Ugh. How could this have got here?'

For attached to the roots of the hair we could make out what was unmistakably a clump of ragged scalp tissue. Tissue that had a fresh, damp look, with slight traces of blood.

And it was human hair. Human hair which must have been forcibly uprooted from the head which had once borne it.

Another sly draught came crawling along the floor and wriggled itself between our legs. And the windows in the sitting-room prattled violently as a savage gust of wind moaned round Eltonsbrody. I shivered and turned my head quickly, for some reason expecting to see the epergne grinning greenly at me out of the musty darkness.

II

It was a lock of dark, wavy hair, and, from its length, I felt fairly certain that it must have been from the head of a man. Despite this conviction, however, and in an attempt to allay her uneasiness, I said: 'Perhaps it was torn from Malverne's head when she fell down here. Nothing to worry about, I suppose.'

She glanced at me. 'Malverne? The patient you mean?'

'Yes.'

She shook her head. 'That couldn't be. Her hair is light-brown. I've got a whole bunch of it on the little table near the bed. The doctor must have clipped it off so as to shave the area of the wound on her head. You've only got to glance at it to see it's different from this.'

I made mumbling sounds of assent. 'Of course—yes. Now you mention it, Malverne's hair is certainly fair—and dead-straight.'

'This hair is dark, and it's got a slight wave. It's a man's hair.'

I tried to laugh nonchalantly. 'It could easily be mine—but if you'll look you'll see that I haven't got a clump missing. Have I?'

She laughed, too—uneasily. 'No. But even your hair is a little lighter in colour than this.'

Silence—then she glanced at me and asked: 'Look here, is anything wrong?'

'Wrong?'

'Well, perhaps I shouldn't say wrong, but—oh, I don't know!' She gave another uneasy laugh and said: 'It may be foolish of me, but, for some reason, the moment I entered this house I sort of sensed everything wasn't as it should be.'

'After the greeting you got from Mrs. Scaife you can hardly be blamed for coming to such a conclusion.'

'It may be that, yes—and yet—well, it's more than that, to be truthful. I suppose I'm letting my imagination run away with me, but the whole house has a strange feel. And look what happened upstairs in the room before I came down for dinner. I could have sworn I caught a whiff of the fluid they use when embalming dead bodies.'

'What? What's that? Fluid they use when embalming—'

'Yes. Oh, I'm sure it must be something else, but it seemed—well, it seemed exactly like embalming fluid.'

I frowned at her, then asked: 'Look, let's hear more about this. Why didn't you mention this before? Where did the smell come from?'

'It was in the room upstairs. The room with the patient. It didn't occur to me to remark on it before. I didn't think anything of it.'

'Can you describe it more exactly? I mean, what sort of smell was it?'

'A sickly smell—and sweetish. I've smelt it often in the hospital-mortuary in Bridgetown when the undertaker's man was at work on some corpse.'

'And you say you had a whiff of this same fluid up there in the room with Malverne?'

'Well, it seemed to be the same, but—well, I must have been mistaken. There's no corpse up there, is there?'

'I should hope not,' I said, grunting.

She stared at me hard, then said: 'I'm really beginning to feel there's something you're keeping from me, Mr. Woodsley.'

I grinned. 'I'm a bad actor. I'd intended not to tell you anything until tomorrow, because I don't want to scare you. Anyway, it looks as if I've gone and put my foot in it.'

Jackman entered at this point, and I turned towards the table and said: 'Shall we finish our dinner?'

'I'm not hungry anymore.'

'Same here. Jackman, you'd better clear away the things. Miss Linton and I have decided we're not very hungry this evening. No reflection on your cooking, of course.'

Miss Linton and I made our way into the sitting-room. I offered her a cigarette, but she said she did not smoke. We stood at one of the eastern windows and watched the yellow blebs of light in Martin's Bay while I told her briefly about the events of the past two days.

She was impressed, but did not appear frightened. 'It does seem queer,' she agreed. 'Of course, we have to remember that she's a very eccentric person. She's known over the island for being eccentric.'

I nodded. 'At first, she didn't even impress me as being eccentric—but these past two days have convinced me she's more than eccentric. The woman is clean round the bend.'

A silence followed. We stared out at the night. Once the window before which we were standing suddenly broke out into a frenzied rattling as though some powerful hand had taken hold of it and wanted to shiver it to bits. The wind whistled in through the crevices with an angry frustration, and draughts twined chilly tentacles about us. The whole house seemed to vibrate under the pressure of the wind. I even thought I could sense the dryish smell of limestone and mortar that, to my fancy, appeared to be seeping out of the walls as a result of the anguished struggle between the wind and the gnarled, resistant frame of the building. The gloom about us had an animated quality, alive with shadows that, if tested, it seemed, might prove more than mere insubstantial shadows, and often I found myself turning round with a slow, uneasy stealth to glance at the epergne on the centre table. Once I saw a filmy wisp swirling about it, pale and ghostly, and I grew rigid, staring. Then I realised that it was only smoke from my cigarette which had drifted across the room.

'I think I'd better be going up now,' she said suddenly.

'You're not very scared, I hope?'

She shook her head and smiled. 'Not exactly scared—but I'm glad you've told me what you know. Now, at least, I know what to expect.'

We were moving across the room and were nearing one of the fluted columns which marked the boundary between the sitting-room and the dining-room when we were brought to a halt by a sound from upstairs. A heavy bumping thud. We glanced up at the ceiling, exclaiming softly, for the sound had come from right overhead.

Overhead was the doctor's old room.

Before we could make any comment we heard a quick scampering of foot-steps, and then a cry angry and impatient. Even through the muffling moan of the wind and the rattle of the windows I recognised Mrs. Scaife's voice.

'I think you'd better wait down here a moment, Miss Linton,' I said—and hurried towards the stairs. But despite my caution, I heard her coming after me.

When I got to the top of the stairs the corridor seemed to envelop me in a gloom that was almost palpable. It swirled like wreaths of black silk. Straining my eyes, I managed to make out a dim figure in white. It was moving silently in a westerly direction as though it had just emerged from the doctor's old room. Then it paused, and Mrs. Scaife's voice said: 'I hope you weren't alarmed, Mr. Woodsley. I'm sure it was most clumsy of me. I dropped my trinket-box.'

'What trinket-box?' I snapped, suddenly nettled. 'That was

no trinket-box that dropped. And it happened in the doctor's old room. Were you in there?' As I spoke I began to advance slowly towards her. But, with a soft sound that might have been a grunt or a chuckle, she moved on, and the next instant had vanished into her old room. I heard the key click in the lock.

Miss Linton had come up and was standing near the door of the room in which Malverne lay. I approached her and said: 'You'd better go in at once—and lock the door. And keep it locked until tomorrow morning.'

'You're in the next room, aren't you?'

'Yes. Call out to me if anything bothers you.'

'I will,' she said, and went in. But the door had hardly closed on her when it opened again. She reappeared and said: 'You advised me to lock the door, but I'm afraid there's no key.'

'No key? But there should be. I'm positive I've seen a key in the lock.'

She shrugged. 'It's not there now.'

'That's funny. Why should she have wanted to remove the key?'

We stood for a moment, irresolute, then she said: 'Well, it's her own house. She's entitled to remove the key if she wants. I'll have to trust to luck I'm not disturbed.'

'Anyway, I'm a light sleeper. You don't hesitate to give a loud call if anything fishy turns up.'

She smiled, seemed about to say something, then changed her mind.

'What's it?' I asked. 'You were going to say something.'

'Oh, I didn't want to mention it, but—come inside a minute.'

'What's the trouble?'

'Come in and see for yourself. I prefer you to detect it without my telling you.'

I accompanied her in, my gaze automatically moving towards the big bed where the bandaged form of Malverne lay. I looked round, frowning, but could detect nothing unusual, and was on the point of telling her so when suddenly the sweetish, sickly aroma struck my senses. I recognised it at once as the same smell I had experienced earlier that evening in Mrs. Scaife's old room. 'You mean the smell. Is that it?'

She nodded. 'Yes. It seems to be coming from that room over there.'

'Which room? Oh. That's Gregory's room.' I moved towards the door that gave into the small room, and found that she was right. The smell was strongest about here. When I tried the door I found that it was locked.

'This afternoon this door was open,' I said.

'Did you come in here and have a look inside the room?'

'I did. Just after we found Malverne at the foot of the stairs. I came up here and made a thorough search. This door was open then, and there was no smell like this, either.'

'What's kept in here?'

'A small bed, a clothes-cupboard with some of Gregory's clothes, a little table with a portable gramophone and an album of records. Nothing else that I know of.'

We heard a footstep behind us and turned.

Mrs. Scaife, in her olive-green dressing-gown, was standing in the doorway regarding us, a slight smile on her face. Her gaze was focused on me. She said: 'I came in to say good night to you, Mr. Woodsley. I trust you will spend a restful night.'

'Very thoughtful of you, I'm sure, Mrs. Scaife,' I returned. 'And can you think of any reason why I shouldn't spend a restful night?'

'None whatever.' She spoke with her old benevolent twinkling humour, but she addressed herself reservedly to me. Not once, I noticed, did her gaze move over to the girl.

I cleared my throat. 'I'm afraid there's a rather annoying smell in this room. Especially in the vicinity of this door. Can you explain it, or suggest how we can get rid of it?'

Her features remained composed. Her eyes twinkled on. 'This house is very old, you know, my boy. If you can call 1887 old, of course. Dear old Eltonsbrody! You shouldn't be surprised it if yields a few odd smells now and again, my boy. That's the privilege of an old house.'

'Quite so. Odd smells and odd bumping sounds. And nasty draughts. Anyway, the point is that this particular smell wasn't present in here this afternoon. And this door was open when I tried it. Now it's locked.'

She smiled. 'Have you given up art for the profession of a detective, Mr. Woodsley?'

'Don't evade what I said. I'm talking about this door. Why is it locked? And why is this smell of embalming fluid about here?'

'Oh, you know it's embalming fluid, then?'

'Yes. Nurse Linton identified it.'

'That was very clever of her. Well, I'm sorry I can't go into detailed explanations, but that smell won't fade for a day or two, so I'm afraid Nurse Linton will have to tolerate it. And as for the door, it will have to remain locked.' She chuckled, as though amused at some private joke. 'You must admit, my boy, that I did warn you to expect unusual events in Eltonsbrody. And, believe me, they aren't over yet. There's more to come. Everything, so far, has gone, more or less, according to plan, but through a little accident—a happily gruesome accident—the programme will have to be extended. Just a little accident—which may not even have been an accident.'

'No doubt you're referring to what happened this afternoon to Malverne. I suppose you're hoping it will prove fatal?'

She wagged her finger at me. 'Probing! Probing again, Mr. Woodsley! You naughty boy. But you're off the track. You're not a good detective. Stick to painting. Of course,' she added, 'the mark is strong on you, but I don't think the time has come yet for you to dabble in deathly deeds. Good night, my boy!' She turned and went out.

Miss Linton looked at me and smiled. 'What mark is this you have strong on you?'

'I'd like to know myself. The woman's potty, I tell you.'

I bade her good night and said: 'If I were you I'd put a chair behind the door and hope for the best.'

'I will do that,' she said.

I left her, and a moment later was on the point of going into my room when the door on the opposite side of the corridor opened a trifle so that a slit of yellow lamplight relieved the utter blackness. I heard a chuckle, and saw Mrs. Scaife's face appear.

Her voice came to me like a quavering groan through the sound of the wind.

'She *will* have to hope for the best, my boy. I'm glad you warned her.'

'What do you mean by that?'

But the door closed and the blackness of the corridor whirled thickly about me again. And the wind moaned dolefully round Eltonsbrody.

12

The night was quiet.

I didn't sleep as restfully as I should have liked, but I did sleep. Once, at about one o'clock, I thought I heard footsteps in the corridor, but when I went out with my electric torch and investigated, I found the corridor empty. On another occasion I was certain I caught faint thudding sounds in the doctor's old room, but when I sat up and listened I heard nothing, so had to come to the conclusion that I must have been dreaming.

When I opened my eyes finally the following morning there were yellowish wisps of cirrus in a pale-blue, watery sky. It was early—my watch said twenty to six—and rain seemed to have fallen not long before, for the trees dripped slowly and with a sound of contented wetness. I kept staring idly at the sky through one of the western windows, and was aware of the smell of leaves and earth in the air, and could hear the peep-peep of the chickens from the poultry-runs and the occasional squawk of a hen or the gobble of a turkey—all peaceful, innocuous noises that had a plaintive, coaxing quality so that the temptation to linger in bed in pleasant drowsiness was almost irresistible. Even the wind seemed to have fallen to a low humming, and once, when I heard a mule-cart—probably laden with canes—moving past along the road with a leisured swish and clatter, a weighty, detached lumbering, I had to shut my eyes, thinking what a lulling sound it was—what a rustic, sleepy sound. It seemed to deaden thoughts of activity and disarm the mind.

However, I was determined to rise early and go down to Bathsheba for a dip in the sea, hence refused to allow enticements of any kind to baulk me.

As on previous occasions during the past few days, I went down past Shepherd's Rest House, and plunged in at a point far from that low, squat rock shaped like a leaning monster with its belly eaten away, and which seems to be reaching out at something in the dark-green roaring waves—a something visible only to its time-clouded, inscrutable eyes.

I must have been ten minutes in the water, which kept buffeting me about and threatening to smash my ribs against the hard, pebbly beach, when on emerging and about to get ready for the next powerful roller, I happened to glance towards the rock-monster and see someone standing beside it staring out to sea. It was a woman, but before I could focus my gaze properly I was lifted off my feet and smothered in a green welter of foam and water.

Emerged again, I looked and saw that it was Mrs. Scaife. She had Walter and Patrick with her on leash. Before the next wave attacked me I saw her bend and release the animals. They went bounding and barking up and down the beach in a gay burst of energy.

Her presence here did not surprise me, for she had mentioned that she sometimes took walks down to the beach with the dogs in the morning; the habit was an old one, she had said. Standing by the edge of the sea always reminded her of her girlhood days in Martin's Bay.

She did not show any surprise when I came out and approached her. She smiled and said: 'Taking an early dip, I see, my boy!'

I nodded. 'And you, I note, have taken an early walk.'

'Yes, I felt in the mood to come down and watch the sea at close quarters. This is my favourite rock. My dear, grotesque old rock.'

'Like a monster with its belly eaten away.'

'An excellent analogy. Yes, a monster—but, a friendly monster. At least, to me.' She uttered reminiscent, old-lady sounds, and for a long interval we stood there watching the huge, curling waves crash down upon the brown, pebble-strewn sand. The colour of blue-green glass bottles, they came one after the other with a deep, savage monotony, intricately convuluted and foaming and thunderous, splaying out a multitude of frothy fingers towards our feet so that now and then we had to back away from their soft, swift, hissing persistence.

Unobtrusively I kept watching her. She took deep breaths of the salt sea wind, and once I saw her turn her head and look at the rock, a smile coming to her lips as though this rock might have been a human friend with whom she shared intimacies that only she and it could appreciate.

Suddenly she began to speak—and she might have been unaware of my presence. She had a trance-like expression.

'One night I followed them here—my father and my brother Ian. They were hunting cuttle-fishes in the pools amid the hidden rocks and reefs just under the water. It was a moonlight night, and the wind was warmish. Large black clouds moved in the sky towards the south and darkened the landscape at intervals when they passed across the moon. I had to dodge carefully from embankment to rock—and stealthily, too, so that Father and Ian might not see me, for Father had forbidden me to come out. The clouds were my friends that night. They kept blotting out the moon at the most convenient moments, and gave me the chance to dash across an unsheltered space from one rock or embankment to another. Once, I remember, a few treacherous pebbles came under my feet and I slipped down a shaly incline for several yards. But even a bruised knee didn't prevent me from going on. That didn't lessen the flaming eagerness in me.' She smiled and nodded slowly. 'Yes, the urge that night was terribly strong—so strong that I simply had to disobey and come after them. The urge to follow them and watch them in the moonlight wading amid the pools and pausing to probe in the holes in the reef. And the breakers kept foaming round them so threateningly, as if at minute . . . at *any* delicious minute. . . .'

She broke off and sighed softly—sighed as though in a deep ecstasy.

'How I did watch them that night—watch them and hope. The hunger in me was really desperate. But nothing happened. When I got to this rock I was so fatigued and nervously exhausted I had to give up and turn back. Frustrated and angry, I had to retrace my steps all the rough two miles back to Martin's Bay. It was a bitter night.'

She smiled again, following with her gaze the two dogs as they raced up and down the beach, Patrick barking furiously and with a futility that sprang from sheer exuberance of spirits, and Walter pausing now and then to sniff at the sand then rear up his head suddenly and dash off after Patrick.

Two black boys—one a freak with auburn frizzy hair—approached us shyly and asked for a cent, and Mrs. Scaife smiled and took two pennies from her handbag and held them out. After they had thanked her and run off, she grunted and commented on the utter poverty of the peasants in this district. 'Poor Michael used to give many of them free attention,' she went on, the trance-like look returning to her face. 'But he was too generous, and, of course, they imposed on him shamefully. They called him out for every trivial or imaginary complaint.'

Silence again—then she wagged her head and said: 'I can

remember the first occasion he came to our cottage. My mother had fallen ill with her kidney trouble. He drove up in a little shaky trap, and I was in the tiny cabin we called a kitchen, watching the trap come up the pathway. I saw him get out with his Gladstone bag and come towards the front door. That was the first time I set eyes on him. It wasn't until six or seven weeks later that *he* saw me and met me for the first time. It was at a bazaar meeting at the Rectory of St. Joseph's. He came in a few minutes late—the meeting had already started, and the Rector was referring to the last bazaar and what a success it had been. Michael entered and seated himself as quietly as he could on the chair nearest the door—fortunately that chair happened to be vacant. But the Rector saw him and paused and gave him a smile and a nod. The Rector was very fond of him.'

Abruptly her expression became cold, grim.

'There were two or three ladies who didn't like him because of his colour. One sitting next to me had coloured blood in her, besides—she was olive-complexioned, but, of course, belonged to the upper middle-class. Snobs, all of them. When Michael came in they tittered behind their handkerchiefs and fans. One of them whispered: 'Good gracious! But isn't he an ugly nigger! Look at that huge, flat nose! And the mouth!' And another—it was the mother of one of the planters who own the private cemetery—whispered: 'But he hasn't a nose at all!'

For a longish while she stood there, her body stiff, her lips set tight. Then the mood vanished. She grunted and smiled. 'They were right, of course, in a way. Michael was certainly no beauty—to look at. But, then, they were not able to see what I could see. He had it clearly defined on the left cheek-bone. Rich and deep-seated.'

'What's that?' I asked.

But as though I had not spoken, she continued: 'Like Gregory's. He might have been fond of Gregory had he lived to see the little chap. But he would have been shocked and horrified if I had mentioned to him that I had seen the Mark on Gregory, too. As he was shocked and horrified on our wedding-night when I told him what I had seen on him—deep and dark and rich on the left cheek-bone.' She sighed as if moved at some satisfying memory.

After another pause, she glanced at me and smiled. 'I can see from your expression, my boy, what's going through your thoughts. You think me a lunatic, eh? Yes, I know. Michael was certain I must be insane. It took him more than two years to realise that it wasn't insanity. At first, I nearly despaired, but eventually I did succeed in convincing him—'

'But convincing him of what?' I broke in, my curiosity overcoming my prudence and politeness. 'You tell me you aren't insane, Mrs. Scaife—and the way you say it I almost want to believe you. But how could you be sane and still indulge in this talk about death and Marks on your husband's cheek-bone and all the rest of it? Last night you said something about my having a Mark, too. What mark is this?'

'The mark of death. About three people out of every ten have it, my boy—and you are one of them. Like Michael and Gregory. Like Tappin and all the other servants in Eltonsbrody. Like myself—though in my case I have it to an abnormal degree. The mark of the destructive lust, Mr. Woodsley. Many of us have it without knowing it. Many of us, deep within, have the urge to kill and glory in the death-agony of our victims. We may be unconscious of this urge, but it exists. In some of us it manifests itself in various harmless ways. For instance, Michael was a splendid surgeon—that was how it came out in him. In you it's strong, too—that is why I took you in as a guest. I loathe and want to destroy all who do not bear this mark, my boy. I adore those in whom the urge is obviously strong. That is how I fell in love with Michael. That is why I took so instant a liking to Gregory. That is why I greeted you so ardently when you came to Eltonsbrody that evening last week and asked for lodging. That is why I treat my servants so well and have such a deep fondness for them. Because they have the Mark. And that is why I detest Mitchell and his wife.

Neither of them has it. Oh, I suppose you may call it a form of madness—but I can't help it. Nature fashioned me that way, my boy. I warned you I was a strange person, didn't I? Death fascinates me as nothing else does. As a girl, I used to follow my father and brother at night because I hoped to see them accidentally drowned or trapped in the reef. My throat would go dry with a desperate hunger to watch things die— even beasts. I can sense death from afar. When I was a girl I couldn't—but as I got older I developed the power more and more. At nineteen it was strong.'

'You mean you're psychic, then? Clairvoyant?'

'Yes—but in a peculiar way. Only in relation to death. I can't foresee events. Only death.' She was silent a moment, then added: 'I can tell you for a certainty that Malverne won't live.'

'Won't live? But—oh, that's nonsense! I'm afraid I have no patience with that kind of thing. It simply won't wash with me.'

'You'll see, my boy. You'll see. No need for us to argue the point. I foresaw her death yesterday, even before the accident occurred.'

She gave a slight start as though rousing herself from a coma. 'But there! How I've talked! I must be going back to the old house. After breakfast I have to go to the cemetery to take some flowers for Michael's tomb. I love that tomb, Mr. Woodsley. It's like a monument to my love for Michael. But you must have guessed that already, eh? It's among my dearest treasures. I'd defend it with my life against vandals. I'm so attached to it—so fanatically enamoured of it—that I believe one day I'll commit murder if I surprise some youngster pelting stones at it or defacing it in any way. One day a year or so ago I nearly did—oh! But how do I talk! Let me be off!' She called to the two dogs, and obediently they came bounding up.

At the breakfast table, about three-quarters of an hour later, I asked Nurse Linton what sort of night she had spent, and she replied that she had nothing to complain of. 'Except that smell, of course,' she said. 'I found it very annoying at first, but after a while I got used to it and hardly noticed it.'

I told her what Mrs. Scaife had said down on the beach, and she agreed with me that it sounded like insanity. She tried to speak lightly, but I could tell that under her outward cheerfulness she was disturbed.

'How's Malverne?' I asked. 'Any improvement?'

'None, I'm afraid. She's still pretty bad. The doctor is coming. He phoned a little while ago.'

At that moment Mrs. Scaife came downstairs—she had had breakfast about half an hour before—and went into the pantry. We heard her talking to Tappin—to-day was Tappin's day for going to Bridgetown to shop—and then a few minutes later she was asking Bayley about flowers. The flowers for the doctor's tomb, no doubt.

A little later, from my bedroom window I saw her moving along the driveway, a bouquet of flowers in her hand. She went out into the roadway.

Doctor Dayton arrived while she was out, and after he had left, Miss Linton came down outside to the goat-pen where I was smoking and chatting with McTurk. 'You asked me to tell you what the doctor said,' she began, smiling as though to allay my surprise at her taking the trouble to come all the way to the goat-pen to tell me (I could sense that the real reason for her coming out to me lay in her nervousness and fear of being alone in the house, and later she admitted this). I accompanied her back to the house, and she said that the doctor thought Malverne's condition showed a slight change for the worse.

'He doesn't think she'll last out the rest of the week.'

We were in the sitting-room. The sunlight was playing on the sideboard, and the glassware flashed and glinted as the foliage of the casuarinas shifted in the wind. The brain-coral smiled up slyly at me, the shadow of a tall flagon lying across its grey hump.

We both turned as Mrs. Scaife entered. She moved past us as though we did not exist, and went upstairs—though there was nothing strained in her expression. She had a quiet, mild air of satisfaction. I am certain she would have given me a cordial reply if I had spoken to her. She was carrying a small hand-basket. It had a cover, and the cover was tightly in place.

'I wonder what she's got in that,' Miss Linton smiled.

'Some graveyard relic, perhaps, who knows!'

A few minutes later, Miss Linton went upstairs, and I went into the sitting-room to finish my cigarette and watch the rugged landscape. It looked cool and slightly misty in the dazzling sunshine. On the horizon I could make out the sails of several fishing-boats. The wind was fresh and filled with the invigorating smell of the sea—and of fish. Fish from yesterday's catch, perhaps, which had left their rank odour indelibly on the landscape.

I went upstairs, intending to get my painting things in order to continue work on my study of Eltonsbrody. But as I was about to pass the patient's room, the door opened and Miss Linton appeared.

'I was waiting for you to come up,' she said. She looked a bit pale and frightened, I thought. 'Would you mind coming in here a moment?'

Wondering, I entered the room with her.

She took up from the table beside the bed a sheet of paper. 'Have a look at this,' she said, and handed it to me.

It was yellowish with age, and there was writing on it—a slanting, beautiful copperplate. It seemed like a leaf torn from some diary, for at the top left-hand corner there was a date— 26th March, 1918.

This is what I found myself reading in the beautiful copperplate:

This time I was disappointed, but it soon fell out that disappointment was to change into ecstasy. As soon as Miss Fletcher arrived I saw she did not have the Mark, and I was furious, but the following morning imagine my excitement and delight when I saw upon her the Shadow! I knew she was going to die; in what manner I had no idea, but I simply knew she was doomed, and it would happen very shortly. I followed her about every moment of the day, hoping, hoping, almost hungry to see her lying dead before me, perhaps

writhing and with her bowels gushing out on the floor, foaming blood
at her mouth and nose, her eyes bulging out of her head, wallow-
ing in her own faeces. Yes, this is the fate I wish everyone who does
not bear the mark of death. Let them suffer, let them groan, let them
writhe, let them shriek, let them gnash their teeth.

13

She asked me what I made of it, and I shrugged. 'Nasty. And
without any doubt the product of an insane mind.'

I turned the sheet over, but there was nothing written on
the other side. I heard her murmur: 'It's Mrs. Scaife's handwriting.'

I glanced up. 'How do you know? Have you ever seen her
handwriting?'

'Yes.'

'I *assumed* it was, of course.'

'What's written there seems to fit in exactly with what
you've told me about her—I mean her queerness. I'm certain
it was intended for me to read.'

'I suppose so. Look, by the way, where have you seen her
handwriting before that you're so certain this is hers?'

'Look on the dressing-table there. That's her cheque book.
I didn't want to be officious, but after reading this thing I
thought I was justified in looking through her cheque-book to
compare the writing on the counterfoils with the writing on
this paper.'

I glanced at the dressing-table and saw the cheque-book. I
moved over and took it up. It was one issued by Barclay's Bank,
and examining the counterfoils, I saw that she was right. The
handwriting was unmistakably the same. The years had not
changed it. Same neat, sloping copperplate.

'But what on earth could have possessed her to leave this
single sheet lying around? Wasn't it on the table before you
came down to the goat-pen to me? Can you remember?'

'No, it wasn't. I'm certain about that. I'd have noticed it. I've been taking up and putting down things on this table from the moment I got up this morning. And just where I found it here near the phone the doctor placed his stethoscope. I would have noticed it at once if it had been there during the doctor's visit.'

'Which means that she must have left it here when she came upstairs a few minutes ago—when she passed us in the dining-room after coming in from her visit to the cemetery.'

'It looks like that,' she nodded.

Suddenly we both glanced towards the bed. Malverne had made groaning sounds. She was shifting about restlessly, her hands clawing feverishly at the bedclothes. She began to mumble deliriously, but her eyes were still shut.

'I don't like her condition at all,' said Miss Linton.

'Sssh! Wait! Listen! She said something. . . .'

We fell silent.

Malverne, sighing and groaning, kept clawing at the bed-sheet. Then her lips moved, and we heard her say: ''E admire me.' A few mumbling sounds. A few more groans, then: 'But Oi froighten when Oi see him.'

Her moans became animated of a sudden, and she pulled down the front of her night-gown to reveal a breast. Miss Linton hurried to the bed, saying: 'Perhaps you'd better go outside, Mr. Woodsley. She's been doing this rather often.'

'Don't upset yourself,' I told her, with a chuckle. 'I'm accustomed to it. It happened when she was conscious, too.'

'When she was conscious?'

'Yes. I was a bit embarrassed to tell you that part of the business,' I admitted. 'But it's nothing new.' And I went on to tell her about Malverne's aberration.

She went a little pink, then laughed and said: 'This is a strange household, isn't it?'

'I agree. But tell me. Is this the first time she's mumbled things?'

'Oh, no. She's been doing that a lot—especially during the early hours this morning. And she keeps exposing her bosom.

I couldn't understand why—but now you've explained—'

'Ssssh! Listen!'

Malverne had begun to mumble again. We heard her say: ''E look at me and 'e smoile. Big ugly, black face!'

'Know who she's referring to?' I asked.

'You mean Borkum?'

I nodded. Suddenly my gaze came to rest on the bookshelf over the washstand, and I remembered something. One of the books was standing at a slant, and there were two dark triangular spaces on either side of it—a clear indication that a volume in that vicinity had been removed.

I went over to the book-shelf, frowning. I remembered how on Sunday night—the night things had begun to go awry in this house—Mrs. Scaife had stood behind me with the lamp, her body rigid, her manner one of breathless, suppressed excitement as I looked over the titles. I remembered the remark she had made: 'All these books were given to me by my husband during our courting days. With the exception of one.' And the following morning at breakfast: 'If you go upstairs and look on my book-shelf—I'm not telling you to do so, mind—you'll find there a volume that might shock you. It would tell you many astounding and horrifying things. It's not a printed book. It's a loose-leaf manuscript enclosed within the covers of a book.'

I felt sure that it was from this manuscript that this sheet we had here now had come. And this space on the book-shelf was where the manuscript enclosed in its mock book-covers had stood.

I shut my eyes and tried to recall the titles I had seen on the shelf on Sunday night. Almost without any effort, and just in a flash, I had it.

The missing title was *Human Anatomy.*

'What was the name of the author?' Miss Linton asked me when I told her. But I had to admit that I couldn't remember. 'It's possible the cover was made by some book-binder in Bridgetown.'

'You mean the title was only a sort of blind?'

'Precisely,' I said.

I wandered over to the dressing-table again, and taking up the cheque-book, began to compare the writing on the counterfoils with that on the manuscript folio—to make quite sure that it really tallied, for somehow I still found myself reluctant to believe that a frail, harmless-looking creature like the mistress of Eltonsbrody could have penned the words on this yellowed sheet. True that she had been forty years younger at the time, a girl in her early twenties, but, if anything, that made it even more monstrous.

I broke off in my reflections.

Flicking through the counterfoils, I had reached the one last written on. I saw that it bore the previous day's date—and the sum involved was a thousand dollars. But this was not what had made me pause and frown. This amount—this thousand dollars—had been made out in favour of one Simeon Borkum.

Miss Linton asked me what was the matter.

'This,' I said. 'Mrs. Scaife has made out a cheque here in Borkum's favour. Didn't you notice when you looked through it?'

'I didn't pay any special attention to the names—only the handwriting. But what's so important about that?'

'It's the last cheque she made out. Yesterday's date.'

'A thousand dollars to Borkum! Yes, I see now. It does seem a bit strange. I wonder why she wanted to pay him all that?'

'I'd like to know myself. I'm going to ask her.'

'You're going to ask her!'

I grinned. 'Seems like cheek, eh? She's accustomed to me by now—and, in any case, she's told me I must never consider it inquisitive to ask her anything about her affairs.'

She said nothing.

On the bed, Malverne began to shift about again and mumble.

I put down the cheque-book and moved over to a window,

stood for a while looking out at the bright morning and listening to the hissing rustle of the casuarinas. The wind droned with unabated steadiness round the house, a thing of unalterable purpose. Malverne mumbled fragments of phrases. She sighed and moaned, her hands clawing at the bedsheet. A whiff of the sickly, sweetish smell of the embalming fluid came to my senses, and my gaze wandered to the door of the small room.

Suddenly, I turned from the window and said: 'Look here, we should do a little talking about this thing, Miss Linton. Do you want to remain here? I mean, after reading this thing, I can well understand if you clear off back to Bridgetown.'

She hesitated, then said: 'I was thinking of phoning Doctor Dayton and asking him to get someone else, but—well, I don't know. He's been very good to me in helping me to build up my practice, and I shouldn't like to walk out on this case because of some imagined threat to my life. I mean, what am I going to tell him? After all, there's nothing really definite to go on. She might be just trying to poke fun at me.'

'I understand. Still, I don't like the way she's behaving. Fun or no fun, it's in bad taste. And disturbing, to say the least.'

She laughed. 'You sound like Sherlock Holmes or somebody like that.'

'Do I?' I felt the blood warm in my face. I chuckled and said: 'I didn't *mean* to sound like a fiction detective. Anyway, you're going to remain, then?'

'Yes, I think so—for the time being, anyway. You're not going?'

'If you hadn't turned up yesterday I'd have gone this morning. The atmosphere of this house doesn't suit me. I don't like mysteries like this.'

We fell silent. The wind seemed to mock us. It gave a sudden whooping whine. And I heard the wardrobe in the doctor's old room creak. Then I glanced outside and saw Mrs. Scaife among the arrow-shaped leaves of the eddo plants in the kitchen-garden. I had an idea.

'I say, she's out there now in the kitchen-garden. See her? Suppose you keep an eye on her for me. I've just thought of something.'

'What's that?'

'I'm going into her room to see if I can find that manuscript.'

'Do you think the door will be open?'

'Well, if it's locked I'm out of luck, of course.'

'All right. Go on. I'll warn you if I see her coming towards the house.'

I left the room and moved west along the corridor. Automatically I found myself looking round to make sure that no one was observing me. Even by the light of day this corridor seemed desperately lonely and forbidding. I felt draughts chasing me, encircling me, tickling my neck as though they might have been wanton invisible presences intent on unnerving me. I heard them whining in under the eaves in the doctor's old room. The wardrobe creaked ominously.

When I tried the door of Mrs. Scaife's old room I found that it was not locked, and grunted to myself with satisfaction, though my heart did give a bit of a bounce at the thought of the manuscript. What new horrible entries would I read?

But I never got as far as glancing into the room. My hand was still on the door-knob when I heard a shriek from Miss Linton.

I turned my head, and she appeared at the door of the room along the corridor. Her face was terrified.

'Mr. Woodsley, come! Quickly, please! Quickly!' she cried out.

14

It's a good thing I have kept those two manuscript folios, for whenever any of my sceptical friends challenge the authenticity of this account I'm always able to produce the two yellowed sheets as evidence that I didn't dream up at least that *part* of the business.

Yes, there were *two* folios (you will hear about the second one in a moment)—the only two, as it happens, I ever succeeded in securing. Even though, afterwards, the servants and I searched everywhere throughout the house, we never found the rest of the manuscript.

What caused Miss Linton's shriek was a rat. My leg has often been pulled about this, many people suggesting, with banal wit, that they were certain it must have been a mouse.

'I heard a soft sound,' Miss Linton told me, 'and when I glanced round I saw a huge rat running across the floor. It gave me a terrific fright. That's why I screamed,' she ended a little naively. She was trembling.

'Where did it come from?' I asked her. 'I can't say I've heard or seen rats here since I've come.'

'I saw it all right, though,' she said. 'It climbed up the facing of the door there and ran along the beam out of sight. I think it must have gone out under the eaves.'

I looked round the room, then my gaze paused at the washstand. It was one of these washstands with a small cupboard built in under the marble-topped section. I noticed that the door of this cupboard was ajar.

'Did you open the cupboard door of the washstand?'

She followed my gaze and shook her head. 'No. Why? I haven't had need to go in there for anything.'

I crossed and pulled the door wide open—and then we saw everything.

It was the second folio. It was pinned up against one side of the cupboard, inside, and on the floor of the little enclosure we could see what looked like a small sack—one of these white canvas sacks in which samples of flour, I believe, are packed, though there were no markings on this one, and it had an old, battered and grimy look. A large hole with jagged edges gaped in the canvas near one end of the sack, and there were bits of the material strewn about. It didn't need a Sherlock Holmes to deduce that the rat Miss Linton had seen must have been sewn up into this sack. It must have gnawed its way out, pushed the door open and escaped into the room.

'But why should she have wanted to do a thing like this?' Miss Linton said.

'Perhaps it's her idea of a practical joke. What else to conclude?'

'She must really be quite out of her mind.'

'What interests me,' I said, 'is where she could have got it from. Not in the cemetery, I'm sure.'

Meanwhile I had detached the folio. Miss Linton came close to me, and, together, we read what was written on it. There was no date, but the copperplate script was identical with that on the first one. It was not until afterwards that I realised that the contents of this folio were a continuation of the diary entry of the other folio.

And knowing that she was going to die, we read, *I went out of my way to torment her. My torment took the form of a series of practical jokes, and before noon I had succeeded in getting her into a terrible state of nerves—that was yesterday—and now to-day she is a corpse. And what a superb death! Falling through the window of the northwestern room which overlooks the old fence. My God! Imagine my joy and horror exquisitely intermingled when I rushed down to find her impaled on a sharp-pointed wallaba post! Her bowels were gushing out just as I had pictured might happen. My bliss was almost sexual! Poor Michael is disgusted because of my reactions, but it can't be helped. I'm glad she is dead—sorry in a human way, but in my own strange way glad to an inordinate degree. And Michael doesn't know I've rooted out two locks of her hair and cut out her heart, kidneys and what I believe to be her ovaries and Fallopian tubes. I'm going to preserve these in alcohol and add them to my little secret collection of 'relics'. Oh, joy!*

'Well,' I said, 'I think this proves it finally. It's insanity. Not the slightest doubt about it now.'

Miss Linton made no comment.

I gripped her arm. 'Look, I hope you're not taking this thing seriously?'

'Seriously?'

'I mean these folios and what's written on them. You don't believe she has the power to sense death from afar or anything absurd like that?'

She gave an uneasy chuckle. 'I should hope not—oh, I know I'm being very silly, but I can't help thinking it seems rather queer. Wouldn't you, in my place, have felt that her object in leaving these folios in here was to let me know I'm in the same boat as the Miss Fletcher she mentions? And look at how she greeted me last night when I arrived! It's almost as if she looked for this "mark of death" on me and didn't find it and so at once took a dislike to me. I won't even be surprised if she thinks she's seen the "shadow" on me, too!'

I laughed. 'This is getting a bit funny!'

'It *should* be funny, you mean. I don't like it. I feel I ought to get out of this house right away.'

'Can't say I disagree with you.'

At this moment the door opened and Mrs. Scaife appeared.

We both started, for we hadn't heard her coming along the corridor.

'I've come to inquire after the patient, Mr. Woodsley,' she smiled at me. 'Any signs of improvement this morning?'

'Why don't you address the inquiry to the proper person? Don't you think Nurse Linton should better be able to answer you?'

This rebuff did not put her out. If anything, it seemed to amuse her. She smiled on, and said: 'Oh, dear! You do remind me so much of Michael, my boy. So full of propriety, but so forthright!'

I grunted. 'Perhaps it's just as well you don't object to my forthrightness, because I have one or two questions to ask you—one or two very forthright questions—and I want satisfactory answers. I don't want any evasions.'

'You don't?' She chuckled indulgently, her eyes affectionate as well as amused as she regarded me.

'I notice you've made out a cheque in favour of Borkum for a thousand dollars. May I ask why you've suddenly decided to be so generous to an old servant?'

She wagged her head. 'Oh, dear! I can see you would never have been a success at Scotland Yard. Why do you think I'd have paid Borkum a thousand dollars out of sheer generosity, my boy? He performed a very useful little job for me—that's what I've paid him for.' She laughed gaily and added: 'It was a gruesome job, and one must pay well for gruesome work.'

'What gruesome work?'

She raised her brows. 'This is astounding! Don't you know?'

'How could I know? What do you mean?'

'After all the clues I've left lying around? A lock of hair on the stairs last night. The smell of embalming fluid. The heavy bump you heard in the doctor's room after dinner last night. Mr. Woodsley! Mr. Woodsley!'

'I take it the rat you left in the cupboard of the washstand there was also meant to be a "clue"?'

'In a way. Just in a way. I got it from a man who specialises in catching rats in the canefields. The planters pay well for rats when you catch them. I had to give this one some chloroform to keep it asleep in the sack. I suppose it must have gnawed its way out when it awoke. Too bad, too bad. Did it scare anybody in the room here?'

'No, it entertained us!' I glared at her and said: 'What's it all about? What are you trying to do? I can't understand what you're after.'

'Mystery, my boy. Mystery. Wouldn't you say that a quiet old house like Eltonsbrody is the right setting for mysterious happenings? For gruesome, blood-curdling goings-on?'

'Another evasion! Look here, Mrs. Scaife, Miss Linton came here at your request. You asked Doctor Dayton to get a nurse to take care of Malverne. When Miss Linton turned up yesterday evening you greeted her in a very curt manner. Now this morning you come in here and leave a folio on the table which was evidently intended for her to see. Then you play this silly joke on her with a rat and leave another folio in the washstand cupboard. Why are you going out of your way to pester her like this?'

'Don't get heated, my boy. I agree with everything you say. It's really shocking the way I'm behaving towards the nurse, but if you'll recall, I warned you I'm no ordinary person. You must always take that into consideration when judging me—'

'That's a poor excuse. Anyway, this won't stop me. I'm going to go on probing until I find out what's at the bottom of this mystery. For instance, that accident yesterday—I'm inclined to think there's more in it than seems apparent. Perhaps if I reported my suspicions to the police it could be rather unpleasant for you.'

She chuckled, and gave me another genuinely affectionate look. 'Mr. Woodsley, the more I see of you the more fond I grow of you. Please don't go threatening a poor old lady like this. Concerning the accident yesterday, it really was nothing but sheer misadventure. I'd never dream of polishing off poor Malverne. She has the Mark on her, you forget? I'd never lift a finger against anyone with the Mark. No, you mustn't go jumping to melodramatic conclusions. It was an accident. Borkum, like the clumsy, prurient fool he is, came out suddenly from the small room there. He happened to peep out into the room here, and when he saw Malverne waltzing round the place with her over-developed bosom exposed he simply couldn't resist sallying forth and making a lunge at her. Poor girl! She was so scared that she rushed like a mad creature out of the room towards the stairs. But the bedroom rug she was holding tripped her up and sent her pitching headlong down. That's all that happened. Borkum told me everything yesterday evening when I was in the doctor's old room with him.'

'Oh! So you admit you were in there! And Borkum, too!'

She wagged her finger at me and made admonitory sounds. 'Didn't I tell you that if you'd only have a little patience I'd take you into my confidence? You're such an impetuous young man—everything like my dear Michael!'

'What was Borkum doing in the doctor's old room?'

'See! There he goes again! Ready to knock my head off! So impatient! I do hope you won't show such impatience when you make love to Nurse Linton.'

'What do you mean by that?'

She uttered a teasing cackle. 'Nothing, my dear boy. Just a touch of senile jealousy, perhaps.' Suddenly there was a sigh in her manner. She began to move towards the door, and I stared after her, too furious to say anything.

As she was about to pass through the doorway she paused. She turned and gave me a sad look. She sighed and said in a murmur: 'Careful. Your heart may suffer grief if you fell in love, Mr. Woodsley, with the Shadow so dark upon your friend.'

15

After we had had a long chat, Miss Linton decided finally to remain. I had advised her strongly to go, arguing that she had a very good excuse. I said I was sure that Doctor Dayton would understand. She agreed at first and was on the point of phoning the doctor when she suddenly changed her mind and said it was too ridiculous, that she would stick it out a little longer. I shrugged, and didn't try to dissuade her—in fact, even persuaded myself that she was right. 'Best thing,' I said, 'is just to ignore her. The more notice we take of her the more she'll be encouraged to try out her practical jokes.'

By afternoon we were congratulating ourselves, for there had been no more incidents. After lunch I accompanied her upstairs, and as we got to the top of the stairs we saw Mrs. Scaife coming out of the room with the patient. She smiled at me and said that she had been making a telephone call, then made her way along the corridor into her old room. Miss Linton had been certain that the old lady had gone in to engage in more mischief, but I remained in the room with her for over an hour and nothing happened. We searched everywhere for booby-traps or other possible devices of an annoying nature, but found nothing suspicious. By four o'clock Miss Linton's nerves were much better, and when six came and darkness began to fall and still nothing odd had happened I had to remark to her that I was getting a little disappointed.

'Just shows how contradictory human nature can be,' I said. 'When things are happening to bother you you grumble, and the moment everything grows quiet you yawn and feel bored.'

'Not me,' she smiled. 'I'm not grumbling about being bored. It will suit me perfectly if things can remain quiet like this.'

The sunset that day was magnificent. Long, flaming feathers of cirrus swept up towards the zenith above Hackleton's Cliff, and in the south and east as well the clouds glowed with bright carmine. The whole landscape lay coated in a weird, wild glare, as though enchanted. The rocks that lined the coast stood out purple-black and with a detailed clarity so that almost every tiny mysterious niche and indentation could be seen. Every hump and tier in the whole jagged descent of the land to the pebbly beach seemed to loom up with a startling and unnatural significance. The canefields looked like soft fairy rugs which had assumed a tint between olive-green and pale violet, and the little cottages dotted here and there on grassy patches might have been umber knobs sprouted from the earth and perhaps soon to dissolve at the gesture of an unseen wand. The sea receded towards the horizon in a hazy purple-blue, broken here and there by the white foam of rollers. It seemed to be the only thing unaffected by the general brilliance, though its very aloofness inspired a sinister awe, and added to the weirdness of the scene.

Tappin, who had just returned from Bridgetown where he had spent the whole day on his shopping visit, remarked to me that this sunset was a sure sign of rain. After we had chatted a bit he asked me how everything had been going in the house during the day, and when I told him about the events of the morning he said: 'Some very bad trouble come on Miss Dahlia, sir. She not de same. Mr. Mitchell, too, very puzzled. Oi drop in to see him to sympathise on Master Gregory's death, and he say he can't understand what wrong wid de mistress.'

'Oh, you dropped in to see him, did you? I've never met him.'

'He's a very noice man, Mr. Woodsley sir. A very noice, good gentleman. Master Gregory's death upset him plenty. After Oi left him Oi went round to de cemetery to see de tomb. It's a very noice tomb, sir—wid a cross and a lil' angel. Mr. Mitchell tell me dat it was Borkum who made de tomb.'

'Borkum, eh?' Something occurred to me and I asked him: 'Did you happen to pass down the street where Borkum has his tomb-making shop?'

'No, sir. Oi seldom passes down dere. But talking about dat, sir, Oi have a joiner friend who keep his shop in de same street not far from where Borkum got his shop. Oi meet him dis morning, and he tell me dat Borkum's shop was closed up all yesterday. He say dat was de first toime for years he ever know Borkum to close up his shop on a working day and take a holiday. It was a joke in de whole neighbourhood, Alfred tell me. Borkum got a ole car, and he and de car left town since Monday, and it was only dis morning Borkum turn up and open de shop again.'

'He has a car, has he?'

'Yes, sir. A ole car. So Alfred tell me. He got some money put aside, Oi hear. Alfred say Borkum come in to a big sum of money some years ago, and it was den he buy de car and open de shop in Tidesdale Street. He live alone over de shop. He not married.'

'You say he came into a big sum of money some years ago? About how long ago would that have been?'

Tappin made a doubtful sound. 'Well, sir, Oi aint too sure, but it must be soon after de doctor dead, because Alfred say Borkum come to Bridgetown to set up shop very soon after Doctor Scaife dead.' He scratched his neck and asked: 'Sir, you suspect Borkum? You think it was he who frighten Malverne and knock her down de stairs?'

'I'm inclined to believe what your mistress told me. He scared her when he appeared from the small room. He peeped in and saw her flaunting her bosom, and couldn't resist trying to make a pass at her. Then she rushed out of the room with the rug, tripped up and fell down the stairs. But what puzzles me is what he was doing in that small room—and in the doctor's old room.'

'Yes, sir, dat very funny. Really very funny.'

I looked past him at the poultry-runs and the goat-pens. McTurk was scolding Bayley for some misdemeanour involving a bucket of water and a fowl-coop, and Bayley kept uttering shushing sounds evidently addressed to the chickens. Scoldings never appeared to worry Bayley.

The colours had by now faded from the sky. The cirrus feathers had melted into the void, and evening was spreading its leaven of sepia amid the foliage of the trees. The wind brought with it a rank, fishy smell—the fishermen must be unloading the day's catch down at Martin's Bay—and there was the bleakness of night in the wind, too—a refreshing sea-bleakness; so much so that more than once I caught myself taking deep breaths. Some insect made a ticking noise amidst a spiky clump of sisal grass which grew not far from the tool-shed, and the tall, slim, flowering stalk that rose out of the clump took on an air of idyllic mystery—a grey-green jumbie-spear pointed up at the darkening branches of the mahogany tree high overhead.

'I think I'll go for a walk,' I said abruptly. 'An evening like this demands that one should be out of doors.'

Tappin smiled, but with an ominous gravity. 'Yes, sir, dat's roight. A very pleasant evening. But dat red in de sky lil' whoile ago mean rain tomorrow—and we need plenty rain, sir. Everybody crying out.'

'You're going home now, I suppose?'

'Yes, sir. Dese past few days Oi don't linger too long in dese grounds. Too much funny matters happening of late, Mr. Woodsley sir. Eltonsbrody was always a house Oi loike very much, sir, but dis past two-three days—Oi! No, sir. Oi don't let noight ketch me here.'

I nodded and told him I could well appreciate how he felt.

A little later, after going into the house to make sure that everything was well with Miss Linton, I set out along the road in a southerly direction. This was the road that would take me eventually to Horse Hill and Hackleton's Cliff, but as I had no intention of going that way, I branched off, after a quarter of a mile or so, on to a track that meandered down into a gully. I skirted several canefields, and it was very pleasant listening to the wind sizzling among the long, slim leaves. One or two canes were in arrow, and the plumes, fluffy and grey-mauve in the twilight, hovered above the pale-green of the fields like petrified smoke. The sweet, earthy-rank scent of dry-weather grass swirled through my senses all the while, and once I came to a halt half-way up a hump of land and cocked my head, hearing only the hiss of the browned, ragged grass in the wind. Above me, at the top of the hump, loomed a gnarled black rock that seemed on the point of rolling down upon me with a deep, savage growl of anger.

The gloom had a gun-metal tint, and glancing up, I saw that stars had begun to appear in the sky which was cloudless and a deep violet overhead—a violet that merged gradually into pale blue as one's gaze swept down towards the west.

Soon I found myself emerging on to another well laid out highway. I saw a car parked on the grass border some distance off, and gave a groan, for I had been hoping that nothing indicative of civilisation would have obtruded itself upon the peaceful scene. Even the road seemed an intruder. However, I consoled myself, it would soon be too dark to see anything at all, and perhaps if I proceeded a little farther east the landscape might prove wilder and rocky and innocent of the smearing touch of man and his machines.

So I crossed the road, and presently was descending into a

grassy depression. After circling two huge squatting boulders, I came upon what looked like a goat-track. It led steeply up towards more boulders. I followed it, and on getting to the top of the rise, discovered, to my surprise, that some way to my left in a westerly direction lay the private cemetery where Doctor Scaife was buried. Beyond it, to the north, stretched an extensive area of cultivated land featuring canes mostly, and in the far distance I could make out vaguely above the trees the roof of Eltonsbrody. A short distance behind me the land rose again in a sudden sheer wall of earth and boulders, jagged and bare. A precarious looking cliff jutted not thirty feet above me. It hung like the shoulder of a giant about to press down and blot me out.

I had just decided to trudge on along a track that led round this prominence when something made me hesitate.

I had been glancing idly over the cemetery when, in the vicinity of one of the tombs in the north-eastern section, I thought I glimpsed a slight movement. It did not alarm me, because the first conclusion I came to was that it must be a dog or some other animal. Just the same I hesitated, for in my present mood everything made me suspicious. My fancy bestowed the most innocent object with sinister qualities. Every rock, shadow or clump of shrubs seemed to conceal some sombre presence of evil—some unknown menace.

It had become very dark now, and the white tombs nestled in ghostly array amidst the ragged grass that covered the ground down in the depression. Beyond them, in the west, rose the steepish embankment immediately above which ran the highway—the same road along which Mrs. Scaife and I had come on Monday morning when she brought me to visit the cemetery.

I stood quite still. In the grass the wind kept up its soft, busy sibilance, and far away to the south a dog was barking —a lonely, detached sound. But these were the only disruptive elements in a silence that seemed to beat around me with the whirring persistence of an invisible bat.

Presently the barking of the dog died away, leaving only the sizzle of the wind in the grass.

About three minutes must have elapsed, and I began to tell myself that it was nothing to trouble about. It must have been a cat slinking past one of the tombs. Or it might be a goat grazing amid the grass down there. Wasn't it a goat-track up which I had plodded a few minutes before? Even where I stood now I could make out one or two pellets of goat dung. A goat must have strayed down into the depression. Soon the owner would be along to look for it.

Despite this line of reasoning, I still stood silent, my senses on the alert. Somehow, I didn't want to believe in my deductions. Some other sense warned me of unusual goings-on not far from where I stood.

The warning was not a false one. Suddenly through the hissing of the wind in the grass a new sound came to my ears. A sharp, light tapping. As though someone were chipping at masonry with a chisel and hammer. It seemed to come from the north-eastern edge of the cemetery.

I cocked my head listening.

It stopped—then it began again.

Deciding that this called for investigation, I crept very cautiously down into the depression. I had to take my time about it because the grass kept lisping under my feet and I certainly didn't want the unseen mason to become aware that I was on his trail.

At length, lying flat on my stomach, I managed to wriggle and crawl my way to the south-eastern edge of the cemetery. I crouched behind a tomb with a black marble cross and ornamental railings. The grass was at least a foot high at this spot, and though it afforded me excellent shelter it created the disadvantage that I couldn't move about freely without making my presence known. It was half-withered grass and the rustle it made was sharp and loud. I had to content myself with lying there and listening.

The tapping was distinct now, and more than once I heard

the grass rustle animatedly as the fellow seemed to alter his position in the course of his work.

Suddenly I was sure I could detect a murmur of voices.

I craned my head above the tomb railings, staring hard in the direction from which the voices came.

The tapping had ceased within the past minute or so. But it began again. It lasted a minute or two longer, then stopped, and I heard the murmur of voices again. Then I saw a light glow—but almost in the same instant it was snuffed out, and I heard an impatient exclamation. A voice snapped: 'You imbecile! What do you want to show a light for!'

It was the voice of Mrs. Scaife.

I was not really amazed. I had got quite beyond the stage where anything about that old lady would have surprised me. All at once it came upon me who her companion must be. I remembered the car I had seen parked on the grass border by the roadway, and I remembered, too, what she had mentioned at lunch-time when Miss Linton and I had surprised her coming out of the room with the patient. She had said that she had gone in to put through a telephone call. It must have been Borkum she had spoken to. She must have been arranging with him to come here this evening.

All sorts of questions raced through my mind. Why had she come with Borkum to the cemetery at this time of evening? What did that tapping sound mean? Were they breaking into one of the tombs? What ghoulish business could they be up to?

The idea came to me to throw prudence to the devil and rise up suddenly, rush round and surprise them at what they were doing. I began to consider this in earnest—but the idea had come too late. Even as I was poising myself to spring up I saw dim shapes moving among the tombs. They made for the embankment.

I watched them ascend the embankment to the road, and a moment later the drone of a car's engine sounded. Headlights stabbed whitely through the gloom beyond the embankment, and I could make out the car as it moved along the road. It swept round the bend and disappeared beyond the canefields to the north of the depression.

Rising, I moved quickly round to the north-eastern side of the cemetery, peering about to see if I could find the tomb they had been tampering with. But in the darkness and with all this thick grass I knew that my chances of success were poor. Doctor Scaife's tomb seemed to be the only one that was well cared for. It was on the western side of the cemetery, at the base of the embankment beneath that dangerous bend in the road, and there was no grass around it. Tappin had told me that he had to weed the spot at least once every month.

Thinking of the doctor's tomb, I had unconsciously turned my gaze in a westerly direction.

I saw Mrs. Scaife. She was moving along the road. I made her out distinctly, silhouetted against the pearl-grey after-glow in the western sky.

Suddenly I remembered Miss Linton alone in Eltonsbrody. And Borkum might be on his way there now in the car.

Giving up the search for the tomb I suspected of being tampered with, I clambered up the embankment and began to walk back towards Eltonsbrody, cutting directly across country so as to avoid meeting the old lady—and also in the hope of getting to the house before she did. Some voice of intuition told me that to-night would not be as restful for Miss Linton and me as last night.

When I was nearing the grounds of Eltonsbrody I saw a car parked by the side of the road under the low-hanging branches of a sandbox tree. In passing, I stopped, struck a match and peered inside. There was nothing of particular interest to see, but I noted it was an old car. The paint had lost its sheen, the leather upholstery was cracked and torn, the wind-screen looked water-stained and cloudy, the bonnet had a dented, battered appearance.

I hurried on, and a few minutes later as I was turning into the gateway of Eltonsbrody, I was certain it was not my imagination when I had a quick glimpse of a dark shape. It seemed to edge away from a clump of crotons that stood just beyond the low hedge that bordered the driveway.

I came to a halt, and kept on looking. And I saw it slink off and vanish among the deep shadows under the mahogany trees.

16

'I'd just begun to think you must have lost your way.' Miss Linton smiled at me when I went upstairs. 'How far did you go?'

'Not very far,' I said, trying to make my voice as casual as I could, for I didn't want her to suspect that anything unusual had occurred. It would only have frightened her and set her nerves on edge again.

'I was trying,' I said, 'to see how far east I could get, but this countryside is much too rugged to wander around in when it's dark. No practical jokes in my absence, I hope?'

'No, nothing, thank goodness.'

We both glanced towards the door as the light footsteps of Mrs. Scaife sounded in the corridor.

'It seems as if she went for a walk, too,' said Miss Linton.

I nodded. 'Quite likely. How's the patient doing now?'

'Still not very good. She's been moaning and talking to herself, and her temperature is a bit higher.'

I took a few paces about the room, feeling aimless—the room seemed rather close, somehow—and then I paused at a window and looked down into the darkness of the kitchen garden. The bark of a dog came, low and gruff. It sounded like Walter.

'The dogs haven't been released,' said Miss Linton, joining me at the window. 'Isn't Tappin or McTurk supposed to set them free every evening before they go home? I think you told me so—'

'Haven't they been set free?'

'No. I saw them chained near the kennel up to a few minutes ago.'

I shrugged. 'Perhaps the old lady will release them herself later.'

We continued to stare out at the darkness. The wind droned round the house, unflagging in its perpetual onslaught on the framework of Eltonsbrody. I felt a draught groping tentatively round my ankle, sending a thin, cold finger up my leg.

Walter barked again, and this time there seemed a note of anger and fear in the sound. We could hear the chain rattling. Then Patrick began to utter whining cries, and eventually howled mournfully.

'Do you think something could be upsetting them?' she asked me.

'Don't think so,' I said. 'They're probably pining to be set free, that's all.'

We fell silent again. Glancing once at her face, I wondered if she, too, were listening to the unearthly whisper of the casuarinas outside. Out of the corner of my eye I could see her hand on the sill. It kept clenching slowly and unclenching.

Light footsteps became evident again in the corridor, then on the stairs. Miss Linton glanced at me.

'She seems to be going downstairs again.'

I grinned and said: 'I can see we're both going to have at least one good creepy story to tell next Christmas Eve.'

'You're right,' she laughed—but it was a jerky laugh.

Presently, we heard the tinkle of a bell downstairs, and knew that Jackman was summoning us to dinner.

A minute later when we were taking our places at the table we heard a footstep in the sitting-room and stiffened alertly, our glances moving towards the gloom beyond the four fluted columns. We saw Mrs. Scaife, a dim shape, crossing the spacious room. She walked slowly as though deep in thought and unaware of our presence in the dining-room here.

Miss Linton smiled and murmured: 'It looks as if I'm not the only one with nerves this evening.'

I nodded. 'I admit it. I do feel hellishly jumpy myself.'

'I hope it's a sign that we'll have as quiet a night as last night. Last night we felt jumpy, too, but—' She had been unfolding her napkin as she spoke. Now she was staring down at her lap, and I saw the colour leave her cheeks. She made a brushing motion on her lap and rose.

'What's the matter?' I asked.

In the sitting-room, Mrs. Scaife had paused at a window and was staring out at the night. Instead of turning my attention floorwards, I glanced towards the old lady, somehow connecting the girl's actions with the presence of our hostess in the sitting-room.

'I don't think I want to eat anymore,' Miss Linton murmured.

'Why?' I asked. 'What's wrong?'

'Look on the floor near my chair,' she said.

I looked down. Something whitish caught my eye. I stooped and picked it up. 'What's . . . ?' I broke off, suddenly recognising what I was looking at. It was a bone—or, better, three bones linked together by fine thread. The phalanges of a human finger.

'Where did this come from?' I asked.

'It fell out of my napkin.'

'I see.'

I glanced again into the sitting-room. The windows made a tremulous chattering as an unusually strong gust of wind attacked them. The flame of the lamp reached for the top of the glass shade, then subsided.

At this point Jackman entered. She looked from me to Miss Linton with inquiring eyes. 'Anyt'ing you need, sir? Miss?'

'No, nothing, thank you, Jackman. If we need you we'll ring.'

She hesitated, then went out, though she paused at the pantry door to glance back curiously at us.

I looked towards the sitting-room. 'Mrs. Scaife!'

The old lady turned at once and began to approach. She was smiling with a sweet, affectionate cordiality as she came past the columns into the full radiance of the lamp.

'Did you call, my boy?' Her voice was caressing, soft, motherly. It seemed absurd to think of her as the sinister figure I had seen silhouetted against the sky not an hour ago.

'Yes, I did call,' I said coldly. I pointed to the bones which I had put down on the edge of the table. 'I'd be glad if you could explain this.'

'Explain? What's that?' She seemed surprised. Then she looked at the table and said: 'Oh.' She took a pace forward and bent her gaze upon the grisly relic. 'Good gracious! Why, it's a little group of bones! The phalanges of a human finger, isn't it?'

Neither Miss Linton nor I made any comment.

Mrs. Scaife uttered soft grunting sounds. She took up the bones and began to examine them with an air of mild, pleasurable interest. She might have been a collector of rare pottery and this was an item that had just been brought to her notice for comment.

'Very nicely strung together, I must say. The work of an expert. Where did you find this, my boy?'

'It was in Nurse Linton's napkin.'

Her brows went up. 'Indeed! Well, well! How odd! And it's the very thing I've been hunting for all day long.'

'It illustrates that you have a very perverted sense of humour, Mrs. Scaife.'

'Me? Me with a perverted sense of humour!' She wagged her head. 'I do wish it were only my sense of humour that was perverted, Mr. Woodsley. Why, I'm perverted through and through. I thought you knew that. I'm an awful person. I always used to warn Michael not to indulge in any under-statements when referring to my vices. Ah, but there! I'm forgetting my manners. Nurse, thank you for recovering this little thing for me. It's a very dear keepsake of a job Borkum and I performed over eight years ago. On the night of the thirteenth of January, to be exact.' She sighed again, this time rapturously. 'Ah! Wasn't that a delicious night! So dreadful—and so delicious!' She nodded and looked at the bones in her hand. 'Yes, I would have been grieved to lose this. Very grieved.'

She began to move towards the stairs, and I glared after her, feeling strongly tempted to rush at her and strangle her.

At the foot of the stairs she paused and wagged her finger at me. 'I can feel you're furious with me, Mr. Woodsley, but never mind! I hope it won't upset your appetite.' She held up the bones. 'Remember we all have to come to this some day, my boy.'

She chuckled and melted into the gloom up the stairway.

The windows of the sitting-room rattled loudly in another strong gust of wind, and Miss Linton shifted her feet uneasily. I gripped her arm and said: 'Look, don't let this get you down, Miss Linton. Let's sit down and eat.'

'I don't feel like anything.'

'Nonsense! You're going to let an old scarecrow like that prevent you from eating? Come on. Sit down!'

After a little bullying I got her to take her place again and make an attempt at eating. 'Anyway, this is my last meal in this house,' she vowed. 'As soon as I go upstairs I'm going to phone Doctor Dayton and ask him to bring another nurse tomorrow morning to relieve me. I'm going back to town by bus.'

'I can hardly blame you. This is really the limit.'

We were silent for a long interval. Then suddenly I noticed that Jackman was at the pantry door watching us. I smiled and beckoned to her, and she approached at once. 'You look worried, Jackman,' I said, trying to speak lightly. 'What's on your mind?'

'Sir, Oi ain' loike how matters happening, sir. Oi 'fraid. Dis house froighten me bad.'

'It does, eh? Have the other servants gone home already?'

'Yes, sir. Only Oi left behind, Mr. Woodsley.'

'What really are you afraid of?'

'Everyt'ing, sir. De way Miss Dahlia behaving particular. She never behave loike dis before, sir.' She took a swift glance at the stairway, then bent in a confidential manner and said: 'Sir, Oi can tell you private. Oi see Miss Dahlia when she put dat bone in de young lady's serviette. Yes, sir. Oi stands jest by dat pantry door and Oi see her come to de table here and do it. She put de bone in de young lady's serviette, and she smile to herself and walk off into de sitting-room.'

'You saw that, did you?'

'Yes, sir. But, sir, dat ain' all what froighten me. Few minutes a-whoile ago Oi was standing at de window in de kitchen washing a pot and Oi hear footsteps outside walking in de dark near de goat-pens. And Oi hear a noise loike ef somebody rest a heavy box on de ground.'

'A heavy box?'

'Yes, sir. Dat's what it sound loike. A heavy box—or a trunk, or somet'ing jest loike dat. Near de goat-pens, sir.'

'Certainly doesn't sound too pleasant.' I said, trying to make my tone as bantering as possible. 'Anyway, don't let it bother you too much, Jackman. When you're ready to go home let me know and I'll come with you to the gate.'

'Many, many thanks, Mr. Woodsley. Oi'd be grateful, sir.'

She was about to move off, but I stayed her. 'Look, just a minute. There's something I was to have asked you. You were here since Doctor Scaife's time, weren't you?'

'Yes, sir.'

'Do you remember if anything strange happened after the doctor died? Very shortly after he died, I mean?'

'Anyt'ing strange loike what, sir?'

'Anything at all you can think of. Think a bit and see.'

She was silent a moment, grunting in a musing way, then said: 'Well, sir, onlyest t'ing Oi can remember was dat Miss Dahlia give us a day holiday. Oi can remember dat.'

'What about Borkum? Wasn't he working here, too, then? Did he take a holiday, too?

'Well, now you talk 'bout dat, sir, Oi remember somet'ing.

Oi was talking to Tappin 'bout it dis morning early on de way to work. Oi got a cousin. She live near Horse Hill, and she used to work at de hotel—de Atlantis Hotel—and she had to pass here every day on her way to work. And Oi remember she tell me dat she pass here and see Borkum working in de grounds. She even ask me ef Borkum didn't get a holiday wid de rest of us.'

'I see. Borkum turned out to work as usual on the day you were all supposed to be off.'

'Yes, sir. And somet'ing else Oi jest remember. Tappin been telling me 'bout de funny smell you and de young lady here been smelling upstairs. Well, sir, Oi can tell you private. Peters, de first housemaid who work here before Malverne, she tell me dat she smell a same funny smell upstairs in de passage-way de day when we turn out to work. Yes, sir. Peters say de smell was strongest outside de doctor's room. For days after she smell it. It take nearly a week to die away.'

'And I take it the doctor's room was locked up?'

'Oh, yes, sir! When we turn out dat day after de holiday both de rooms over dat side lock up. From dat day dose two rooms never open. Never not once! And de mistress tell Peters dat why she lock dem up is so as to give Peters less work in cleaning up.'

'Why did Peters leave Eltonsbrody, by the way?'

'She get a better job in Bridgetown, sir.'

'You're quite certain it was on the day after the holiday that Peters first began to smell this funny smell?'

'Yes sir. Oi sure 'bout dat. Soon as we turn out to work.'

'That would be two days after the doctor's death?'

'Yes, sir.'

'Thank you, Jackman. Interesting to hear about these little things. Well, don't forget. As soon as you're ready to leave just come and call me. I'll be in the sitting-room.' A little later, after seeing Miss Linton upstairs and searching the room to make sure that nothing odd had been planted anywhere during our absence, I returned downstairs and settled down in the one comfortable chair in the sitting-room to smoke and wait for Jackman's call.

The draughts, as usual, did not leave me alone. They circled about my head, crawled up my trousers legs, shivered their way down my neck, and the windows kept up their spasmodic rattling as the wind pushed at them. My old enemy, the epergne on the centre table, kept slithering into my range of vision, tantalising, elegant and ghostly. Now and then it would become merged with a drifting puff of smoke from my cigarette, and in these moments it seemed to smile and nod at me behind the uncertain temporary veil.

I was relieved when I heard Jackman's footsteps in the dining-room. She said she was ready to go, and I accompanied her out through the kitchen door. The back garden was dark, but my eyes soon grew accustomed to the darkness as we moved round the side of the house along the pathway that led to the front garden and the driveway. The dogs barked and whined in their kennels, and Jackman said that her mistress had told McTurk not to release them. I made no comment, and a minute later wished her good night and stood at the tall iron gate watching her go out of sight along the road. She lived about half a mile away, she had told me.

It was good inhaling the fragrant night air. Now and then a leaf from the mahogany trees would brush past me in the wind and make a light lisp as it skimmed along the ground before coming to rest.

Instead of returning into the house, I went round in the direction of the goat-pens. Flashing on the electric torch I had got from my room after dinner, I brought the beam to bear on the ground everywhere in the vicinity of the poultry-runs and the goat-pens.

Walter and Patrick began to bark with renewed vigour, straining at their leashes. The kennels stood only a few yards from where I was.

Ignoring them, I kept playing the beam of my torch here and there along the ground. But I could find nothing suspicious. The ground was hard and dry, and it was useless to look for impressions. I doubt whether 'a heavy box' made even out of lead or iron would have left any marks.

Still not satisfied, I turned my attention to the track that led through the kitchen garden towards Tappin's tool-shed. I glanced from side to side, flashing the light of the torch on at frequent intervals. Once I thought I heard a sound behind me and, glancing back, nearly walked on to a bed of lettuce. A sense of uneasiness crept over me as I went on. The star-light was bright, and I could make out the track without the aid of the torch, but it gave me more confidence to keep playing the beam about.

An insect clicked and made a swift arc through the light, and it startled me so much I had to come to a halt. The inclination to turn back and make a dash for the house was almost overbearing.

Suddenly Patrick began to howl, taking a high, mournful note that seemed to end on a human-like groan, and I found myself remembering that dogs were supposed to be psychic and could sense the presence of death. Was Patrick howling because he could divine what I could not?

I was passing the cassava plants now. Their slim, knotted stalks looked like night-black skeletons on my right. Had they begun to hop and skip about in a silent dance of death I think I wouldn't have been very surprised. Anything macabre seemed possible at any instant.

I emerged into the clearing where Tappin's tool-shed stood. The sight of it reassured me. Tappin's goodnatured aura seemed to hang round it, dispelling evil influences. The mahogany tree, too, nearby inspired me with confidence. Its weathered trunk had a look of solidity and safety. It seemed contemptuous of everything sinister and phantasmal.

I flashed the light round the clearing. Nothing terrifying to see. Yet my uneasiness began to return. Some sense warned me that I was being watched, warned me to be on the alert.

Tingling all over, I moved round behind the tool-shed. My

foot stumbled against something that gave out a dull, hollow thud. I looked down and saw what it was.

On the leafy ground, pushed right up against the rear wall of the shed, was a rough wooden coffin.

17

Above me the foliage of the mahogany tree hissed in the wind as at any other time, but to my fancy at this moment the sound had a special significance. It was like the rasping breath of a ghoul perched on the limb right above me.

Steeling myself, I reached forward and lifted the lid of the coffin.

It was empty. There was no corpse in it as I had dreaded. But something else that caught my attention increased my uneasiness. On the ground near the head of the coffin there was a Gladstone bag, old and very battered looking. It was half-open, and the beam of my torch revealed inside it a collection of surgical instruments. I stooped and opened the bag wide. Just inside, under the middle catch, on a worn silk lining, I read in faded gold letters the name *Simeon Borkum*.

In the bag I recognised two scalpels, forceps of different sizes, a surgical saw, catheters, a dissector, a gouge.

I did not wait to investigate further. I hurried back towards the house, deciding that I must see Mrs. Scaife at once about my find. My nerves were in a ragged state now or I might not have acted in this precipitate manner. I dashed up the stairs three at a time.

Miss Linton was at the door of the patient's room, apparently awaiting me. But I hardly gave her a glance. I flew past and charged up the corridor to the door of the room which Mrs. Scaife now occupied.

I hammered on the panels, noting that a yellow streak of light showed under the door. The door opened at once. Mrs. Scaife was in her olive-green dressing-gown. She gave me a look of surprise. 'What's it, Mr. Woodsley? Where's the fire?'

'Look, I've found something, Mrs. Scaife,' I said, panting from my exertions. 'I was having a look behind the tool-shed.'

She recoiled slightly. 'Don't tell me it's a murdered corpse you've stumbled upon, Mr. Woodsley!'

'This is no time for fooling,' I snapped. 'There is a coffin behind the tool-shed. And a Gladstone bag with surgical instruments near it.'

She smiled in her old twinkling, affectionate manner and exclaimed: 'What a young man you are for investigating! Good gracious! What next won't you discover! A coffin, indeed! *And* surgical instruments! I congratulate you, my boy! Well done!'

'I think I told you I'm serious!'

'Surely you don't expect *me* to take you seriously. A coffin behind the tool-shed! And a Gladstone bag of surgical instruments! No, please! This is too much for a poor old lady with bad nerves!' She wagged her head and sighed. 'Good heavens! What is Eltonsbrody coming to that coffins are going to appear within these grounds! *And* surgical instruments!'

'Would you be so good as to accompany me outside to the shed?' I said, deciding to call her bluff. But she showed no dismay. She said: 'Why, certainly, my boy! Certainly. With pleasure. You won't have to drag me along. I love coffins. And surgical instruments are my playthings. Haven't I told you how fond I am of cutting up dead bodies! Come, let's go.'

I admit I felt something of a fool as we began to move along the corridor in the direction of the stairs. I saw Miss Linton staring at us, troubled and frightened looking, and this did not help to decrease my discomfiture. 'Any objections if I came along, too?' she asked.

'Well, I don't know . . .' I began, then said: 'All right. Might as well. Only for a few minutes.'

I could sense that the idea of being left alone in the house did not appeal to her.

I led the way along the track to the tool-shed, flashing my

torch about as we went. Mrs. Scaife kept indulging in banter-ing remarks, but I took no notice of her. I was too angry and puzzled. Her manner baffled me. I had expected her to show alarm, or confusion of some sort.

'Well, here we are!' she exclaimed as we emerged into the small clearing where the shed stood. 'I do hope the corpse will have appeared by now. After all, a coffin ought to have a corpse to go along with it, oughtn't it, Mr. Woodsley?'

Without replying, I led the way round to the back of the shed.

But the coffin had vanished. And so had the Gladstone bag.

Mrs. Scaife, as only to be expected, uttered clicking sounds of deprecation and wagged her finger at me. 'Now, what wild-goose chase is this you've brought us on, my boy! Where is the coffin?'

'Perhaps you can tell us that!' I barked.

'I! But wasn't it you who came rushing into the house with the news?'

'You don't fool me. You know all about it.'

'Really, I wish I did. I seldom have the good fortune to find coffins. Was it a pretty one with nickel-plated fittings?'

'What about surgical instruments? Do you seldom come upon those?'

'Oh, no. There's Michael's set—and a very fine set it is. I often take them out to have a look at them, and to imagine myself carving up some succulent dead body.'

'So your late husband's surgical instruments were never disposed of after his death?'

'Good heavens, no! I kept them. I not only kept them but I've taken great care of them. Surgical instruments fascinate me. I've used them myself. Only the night before last I did a very neat little job with them—though please don't think me conceited. Borkum assisted me. He brought his own instru-ments. Oh, we had such fun on Monday night!' She smacked her lips and murmured as though half to herself: 'We might even have some more to-night if we're lucky!' She squeezed my arm and laughed softly. It was a sound of genuine amusement. I could detect nothing sinister in it.

Standing there, I felt a perfect and complete ass.

Miss Linton said: 'Mr. Woodsley, did you really see a coffin—and surgical instruments behind this shed?'

'As plainly as I see you in this beam of light,' I told her. 'I didn't dream it. The instruments were in a Gladstone bag—and the name embossed on the lining inside the bag was Simeon Borkum.'

Mrs. Scaife uttered more deprecatory noises. 'Borkum is an extremely careless fellow. Indiscreet, clumsy. Oh, it's really terrible! If he isn't dropping leaden boxes with human remains so as to cause heavy bumps on the floor he's scaring innocent housemaids or strewing freshly plucked locks of hair on some stairway. I'm going to give him a severe scolding. Not that it will make much difference. He's incurable.'

She gave me a droll glance and went on: 'Yes, he's a case, my boy. I'm always warning him not to leave his instruments lying about. One day he'll lose them, and then I'll see what he'll do!' She glanced at Miss Linton. 'He's an expert dissector, you know, Nurse. Had three years at Edinburgh University. Oh, yes. He simply adores cutting up dead bodies—it's his chief weakness. He has the Mark deep on him, of course, so it's not surprising. In fact, I won't at all be amazed to learn that he's planning one or two murders to-night. If so I hope he lets me know, for I'd love to help him slice up a limb or two.' She sighed and added: 'Perhaps he was only pulling my leg, but once he did confide in me that he has a partiality for female bodies. Dismembering them, I mean.' She squeezed my arm again and tittered. 'Shall we return to the house now, Mr. Holmes?'

Back in the house, I accompanied Miss Linton into the room with the patient, and for a while we discussed the situation.

'I'm seriously beginning to think she's doing this to pull our legs,' I said. 'I can't see what else could be behind it. It doesn't make sense.'

'Anyway, I'm not putting up with it,' she said. 'I'm not fond of jokes that have to do with coffins and human bones. I'm leaving tomorrow morning—that's definite.'

'Have you 'phoned Doctor Dayton already?'

'Yes. I've asked him to come tomorrow morning and bring another nurse. I told him I'd explain fully when I see him in person.'

'I'd like to travel back with you, but I'm a determined sort of blighter. I don't give up easily. I mean to find out what it's all about, and you may be sure I'm going to.'

'Personally, it's no mystery to me. I know the solution already. She's out of her mind. That explains everything.'

'I try to keep telling myself that, too,' I said. 'But somehow I still feel inside me she's not quite as potty as she seems.'

She made no comment, and for an interval we sat immersed in our own reflections, with the moaning wind as a background accompaniment. Now and then Malverne, on the bed, would stir slightly and groan or mumble. My gaze kept straying often to her pale face. Once or twice a whiff of that sweet, sickly smell came to my nostrils, and I'd find my gaze moving across to the locked door of the small room.

Outside in the road, a mule-cart lumbered past, lulling and with a rustic note of reassurance. Hearing it and envisaging the load of canes it carried, I forgot for the moment my grue-some thoughts. Instead, the first three days of my stay in the house came back to me, and I remembered my exploring jaunts down in Martin's Bay and Bathsheba and even as far west as a place called Cattlewash. I remembered the fisher-folk and farmers in their tiny cottages dotted over the landscape. Certainly nothing sinister or suspicious about them. I had talked to quite a number of them, and had succeeded in not seeming too unapproachable, so that they had lost their shy-ness and discussed their occupations—and their struggle to exist on the sparse means that Nature and their own ingenu-ity supplied. Perhaps even at this moment the darkness of the pebbly beach was splotched with the ruddy glow of torches as the menfolk waded out on to the reef and amid the rocks to hunt for crabs and lobsters and cuttle-fish. Mrs. Scaife herself had told me something concerning their methods. As torches they used pieces of rubber cut from old tyres. They tied these to poles, set the rubber afire, and holding the torch aloft, waded out. More than once I had stood at a window in the sitting-room and watched the shuddering blobs of fire travel along the shore, die out, then come alive again in the distant wind-swept dark.

I remembered, too, the Well Pit, the crevasse over which the sea boiled day and night—the spot where boats were sometimes sucked down, never to come up again or be seen— and this thought seemed to align itself with the troubled atmosphere of uncertainty and menace in Eltonsbrody this evening, so that once again I found myself glancing round the room uneasily.

Before leaving her, I gave Miss Linton the same caution as the night before. 'Just let out a good shout and I'll be with you,' I told her. 'And put a chair behind your door.'

'You needn't worry,' she smiled. 'If anything comes in here to trouble me they'll hear me screaming all the way down at Bathsheba.'

Closing the door after me, I stood in the blackness of the corridor listening to the wind and letting the draughts frolic and run riot round me. The one window at the western end was shut, as it had been from the first evening I had arrived in the house. Occasionally a leaf from the mahogany trees would be blown against the clouded panes, and when this happened there would be a flicking sound as though some spectral finger had tapped on the glass.

Mrs. Scaife had evidently retired, for the streak of light under her door was no longer there.

I moved round the well of the stairway and approached the door of the doctor's old room. Somehow, I could not go into my room in this tame way and settle down for bed. I felt I had to do something, potter around a bit, listen, probe, keep my senses cocked.

I stood for several minutes outside the door of the doctor's room listening. Listening and waiting.

The old wardrobe creaked more than once, but I had got too used to that to be seriously affected by it.

Downstairs the windows kept rattling often as though the wind stretched out hands, salt and sea-clammy, and shook them in fierce tantrums. This disturbed me, made me wriggle and shudder even though I tried to deafen my ears to the sound.

Outside, the dogs had grown quiet, so that now the wind and the trees and Eltonsbrody remained the only disrupters of the night silence.

I was gazing down into the inky gloom of the stairway when the new sound came to my hearing.

Perhaps I am wrong in describing it as new, for it had its origin within the house and might have been a very old sound. This banister might have heard it many a time—especially when the doctor was alive. But to me standing there in the draughty corridor, with the dark swirling round me like funereal swathes of crepe, it was no ordinary sound. It was new to me.

It came either from in the doctor's old room or from somewhere in the cut off portion of the corridor that was now the small bedroom. I couldn't be certain because the wind warped and muffled everything, played tricks on the hearing. And what was more, it was a dim sound—so dim and intangible that I had to cock my head and strain my senses to convince myself I was really hearing it and not imagining it.

I heard it again.

A frail metallic clink. Soft but clear and with a sharp ring. Not a musical tinkle but a flat, brittle click and clink. It made you think of someone fumbling in a drawer of cutlery with great care.

Either in the doctor's old room—or in Gregory's.

Then it stopped. And even though I stood there stiffly alert for several minutes I didn't hear it again. Only the wind I heard. The wind. Just the wind whooping now, moaning now, whining in under the eaves, shaking the windows downstairs.

18

It was a weird night—and an exasperating one.

After my fruitless pottering about in the corridor, I went into my room but didn't get into pyjamas at once. I sat by the window smoking and trying to read. More than once I got up, crossed to the door, opened it and had a look up and down the corridor. But there was never anything except the draughty darkness—never any sound but the wind outside and in the windward rooms—or the creaking of the wardrobe against the background of the wind. Or the rattle of the windows downstairs. Tappin must have taken away the canvas sacking from the pantry window, for I didn't hear the usual flap-flap that mimicked so closely the sound of stealthy footsteps.

On two occasions I simply stared at the door of Mrs. Scaife's room directly opposite mine, expectant and tense. And once I even tiptoed silently across and stood listening. Another time I moved along the corridor and listened outside Miss Linton's door.

At length, I got into pyjamas and put out the lamp. But I couldn't sleep. I kept seeing that coffin behind the tool-shed, and the Gladstone bag with the surgical instruments. I knew for a certainty that Borkum was somewhere near. I knew that it must have been he who had taken away the coffin after I had dashed back to the house here to tackle Mrs. Scaife about my find. He must have been waiting about somewhere in the vicinity of the tool-shed watching me and perhaps alarmed at my investigations.

Then I began to ask myself why he should be at Eltonsbrody to-night. I recalled what the old lady had said about liking to cut up dead bodies and about the 'little jobs' she and Borkum had done together. On the night of the thirteenth of January, eight years ago, she and Borkum had done one of these jobs. That would have been the night after the doctor's death. And then there was the thousand dollars she had paid to him a few days before. And from what I could adduce from the odds and ends I'd heard from Tappin, it seemed certain that Borkum had been paid a similar sum shortly after the doctor's death, too. Could there be any connection between the doctor's death eight years before and Gregory's on Monday last?

I must have dozed off at this point. The next thing I knew was that I was staring round into the darkness with a wide-eyed alertness. I flashed on my torch and looked at my watch. It was ten minutes to eleven. It had been five to ten when I put out the lamp.

I sat up and listened.

The wind. The droning and whisking and whining.

And Malverne moaning and mumbling.

I lit the lamp and looked round the room again.

Pale blue walls, the plaster in places cracked and flaked. My gaze paused at one crack. It wriggled like a river on a map out of sight behind the big wardrobe. The desire to get up and see if anything were behind the wardrobe took hold of me, but I told myself not to be absurd and sat where I was.

Suddenly I got up and crossed to the door, pulled it open and looked out into the corridor.

There was a streak of light under Mrs. Scaife's door.

A leaf from one of the mahogany trees flicked against the window at the western end of the corridor. The wardrobe in the doctor's room creaked.

I swore softly. All the old creepy effects! A feeling of monotony and weary pointlessness came upon me. Wind and old wardrobe creaking, windows downstairs rattling, leaf against the window. It was getting tiresome now. My nerves were beginning to protest.

It was I myself who was making a mystery out of nothing, I tried to scold myself. I had let myself build up a whole situation of doubt and intangibility out of the incidents of the past few days, out of what was probably only the eccentricity of a flighty old lady. This house was the ideal example of the romantic haunted house, and Mrs. Scaife was aware of this, so she must have hit on the idea of providing macabre entertainment for me.

I withdrew into the room and shut the door.

I got back into bed and blew out the lamp. But my head had hardly touched the pillow when I heard something that made me sit up again, stiff and alert.

For the second time I heard it. The wind did its best to muffle the sound, to warp it, but my ears caught it just the same.

A sharp metallic clink.

I hopped out of bed, went to the door once again, and put my head out into the dark corridor.

Only the wind. But I waited and listened.

From the room opposite I heard a soft swish as of some sort of cloth material being moved—of some garment being shifted or pulled off. Then nothing. Only the monotony of wind, wind.

Suddenly it came again. The swish of cloth. And then a clink-clink. As though someone had put aside a pair of scissors—or some surgical instrument.

The draughts whirled around me, shooting up my pyjamas legs. I shivered—either from being chilled or from horror and fear.

I tried to convince myself in favour of the chill, because I still wanted to fight shy of taking the thing seriously. It was leg-pull. The old lady was doing this to lead me up the garden path. Tomorrow morning she would have a good laugh at me.

Again I heard the sound. A clink . . . Now there was a tiny tinkling splash of water. And another of those swishing noises, as of some cloth material being shifted.

Silence followed. The silence seemed to waver and fold itself about me like sylph-like gowns trying to smother me.

Suddenly—a new sound. A continuous sound. A lisping and grating. Something was being ground down or cut. Sawn. I remembered the Gladstone bag. There had been a saw among the surgical instruments.

It went on—swift, almost with a whine.

The impulse to rush across the corridor and hammer on the door came upon me. It began to develop into an obsession. Yet I held back. I thought: Suppose it really were some loathsome orgy I barged in upon, then, in desperation, they might murder me to protect themselves, to prevent me turning evidence against them. Or suppose it were a harmless eccentric hobby Mrs. Scaife was indulging in, then she would open the door and wave her hand and laugh. 'See! Only a fret-saw, my boy! Not a corpse as you imagine. Ah, what a young man you are for investigating!'

I should want to hit her hard if it proved only a joke.

I swore to myself, and returned into my room. Went back to bed.

Every now and then I raised my head and listened. But I heard only the wind. And the casuarinas. Once I was certain I caught a whiff of ether, but dismissed this as pure imagination. It was probably the smell from the small room.

At length, I dozed off and had a nightmare. I strode through the wall into the corridor. The walls were translucent. A violet light enveloped everything and through it I saw into the doctor's old room. I saw a pile of surgical instruments on the floor. Scalpels and catheters and saws and gouges and forceps. The forceps worked like the bills of birds and seemed determined to devour the scalpels which, in turn, slashed back furiously, glinting with bloody menace. They made a terrifying tinkle-jingle. Then a shroud of silk slowly swished over the lot and they grew still and silent, anaesthetized. Mrs. Scaife appeared and gave a deep curtsy. She smiled at me and said: 'See! Only a magic shadow-show, my boy. Played in a box whose candle is the moon. The phantom-figures are in your own fancy!' She vanished and the shroud swished aside to reveal a coffin piled high with the phalanges of human fingers. They overflowed in a rattling cascade.

I woke with a feeling of suffocation. Downstairs the windows were rattling in a strong gust, and a draught tickled the soles of my feet.

I realised the room was not as dark as it had been when last I had seen it. There was a violet radiance upon everything. The moon, of course. The moon had risen. The time was twenty-five past twelve.

I got up and went to one of the southern windows. Looked out and saw the trees glittering in the lovely moonlight. The fragrance of leaves and earth came up strongly on the air. The casuarinas made silvery feathers against the sky, and somehow their mysterious wheezing rustle did not seem uncanny now. Their shadows lay upon the kitchen-garden, though here and there an eddoe leaf glimmered, caught in a probing shaft of blue-green light. In the south-west, Hackleton's Cliff rose in umber majesty, stern but not jagged and forbidding as when the harsh light of day revealed its gnarled bulk. Now in this midnight moon-drenched atmosphere it had a velvety, mellow unrealness; it was impressive without being obstrusive; sombre rather than threatening.

I could have stood there indefinitely watching the moon weave intricate prongs and pointers through the trees, but behind me was Eltonsbrody—and I was brought back to actuality by a slight sound that seemed to come from the stairs.

I stood still, listening.

It did not come again, but my fears began to return. I moved to the door, opened it and looked out into the corridor.

The streak of light under Mrs. Scaife's door had vanished. I could hear no sounds from within the room. Then I wrinkled my nostrils, certain I could smell blood. A fresh, rankish smell.

The sound came again on the stairs. A soft bump. Or it might have been down in the dining-room. As though something heavy had collided with the banister or with the sideboard.

I waited, listening hard.

I heard a murmur of voices. Downstairs in the dining-room.

I turned and darted back to the bed, snatched up my torch. I had intended rushing downstairs to investigate, but in my nervous excitement the torch in my hand flashed on accidentally. The beam shot across the corridor, and I saw that the door of Mrs. Scaife's room was slightly ajar. Curiosity attacked me at once. Before going downstairs I must take a peep into the room. And there was the smell of blood. It was still strong. Perhaps it was coming from in there.

I moved quickly across and entered the room.

The rank smell of fresh blood assailed me in full force. The beam of my torch settled on something in the middle of the room. The old-fashioned flat-topped travelling-trunk, formerly under one of the two western windows, had been hauled into a position that brought it nearer to the bed and the door. It stood on the section of floor space between the bed and the chest of drawers, and a surgical sheet had been spread over it. This sheet had very recently been wiped clean, and wet stains darkened the floor round the bottom of the trunk.

I remembered the last time I had been in the room here, remembered the clean oblong patch I had seen on the floor just about where the trunk now stood. Suddenly I knew what had caused that clean patch. It was this trunk. And the stains round the patch had been caused by the fluid that had dripped off from this rubber sheet.

I flashed the beam round the room.

On the wash-stand I saw something that interested me. In an enamel surgical tray with water that looked pinkish-brown lay two scalpels, two surgical saws and a dissector.

The smell of blood persisted strongly.

I continued my search. The bed was still draped with cobwebs. The shifty beam of light made ghostly shadows flicker on the white cupboard as it passed through the dense network of cobwebs. I lowered my hand. The beam flashed upon something white under the bed. I took a pace forward, then drew back with an exclamation.

I was looking into a pail—a white enamel pail—and it was nearly two-thirds filled with thick, fresh clots of blood.

19

Even now the idea still lingered that I might be the object of a huge practical joke. As I hurried out of the room and into mine I asked myself why should it necessarily be human blood? Why couldn't it be that they had been dissecting a goat or two or three rabbits for the purpose of getting that blood to fool me? And mightn't she deliberately have left the scene set in there so that I could go in and come to alarming conclusions? The door had even been left ajar. She might have been keeping a check on my movements and had seen me peering out into the corridor and prowling about.

I began to pace about in the dark, smoking. I paused once at one of the two western windows and frowned out at the moonlight, my head in an ache of confusion.

From this window I could look down on the driveway and the front garden which the moonlight had converted into a real goblin-dell of shadows and uncertain splotches of colour. Simply to stand here and look at it soothed me and eased the throbbing in my head.

The plumbagoes looked like pale blue coins of mist that might dissolve at any instant, and an arbour of bougainvillea was a foaming mass of shadowed crimson. The croton clumps, yellow and red and green and brown, glittered in the moonlight with a secret loveliness that seemed the mere superficial manifestation of richer wonders concealed within the core of their dense foliage. There were roses in tubs, and dahlias, beds of zinnias, a hedge of bell-shaped pink hibiscuses. In this scene I could find nothing that might suggest blood-curdling deeds.

I sighed, telling myself that the whole trouble lay in me myself—in my morbid imagination. Tomorrow morning, I decided solemnly, I would have to do something to recover my 'face'. I would have to let the old lady know by some means that I had twigged her game, that I had seen through her little jokes. I would tell her that murderers did not advertise their premeditated acts in the way she had been trying to fool me she had been doing, that homicidal maniacs were not in the habit of revelling openly in their lust for butchering as she had been pretending to do. I would turn the laugh on her and make her feel a fool for a change.

As though in answer to these reflections, I heard a crunching sound on the driveway. I looked down.

Moving towards the gate was the huge, ungainly figure I had seen in the cemetery. Borkum. He was bearing on his shoulder a long, dark object which I recognised at once as a coffin. Behind him walked Mrs. Scaife. They must have left the house through the front door. That dull bump I had heard on the stairs a short while before must have been caused by the coffin. They must have been taking it down even as I had been hesitating whether to investigate downstairs or to go into the room across the corridor. What had they brought it upstairs for? What was in it now?

I felt an urge to hurry into my clothes, to go rushing after them and demand to be shown what was inside the coffin, demand an explanation of their actions. But this impulse passed almost in the same instant as it came alive. I could tell that it would be futile trying to go after them now. Long before I could catch up with them they would have got to the car waiting by the side of the road. The best policy would be to lie low and just watch things. And who could tell if this coffin business was not part of the practical joke? Perhaps she had guessed I would be looking out of my window to see Borkum take the coffin away.

I heard the car's engine start up. It went droning off along the road.

The rest of the night was spent in spasmodic dozes, sudden awakenings, more investigations in the corridor, vigils at the

window. Mrs. Scaife and Borkum returned at shortly after two
o'clock—my watch said seven minutes past two when I saw
them turn into the driveway—and this time Borkum's arms
were free. The coffin had been disposed of. Could they have
sealed it up within one of the tombs they had been tampering
with some hours ago? But surely that would be taking the joke
too far!

I shrugged and went back to bed.

I got up finally at a quarter to six, changed into bathing
trunks, my head heavy and throbbing, and went out and down
to the sea.

After a refreshing bathe, I plodded up to Staden Hill again
but did not enter the grounds of Eltonsbrody. I went past and
headed for the cemetery. On my way I stopped to take a look
at the old car parked under the branches of the sandbox tree.
As on the evening before, there was nothing of interest inside
it. I searched for blood-stains but failed to find anything that
might resemble dried blood.

At the cemetery the shadows of crosses lay long and distorted amid the half-dry grass, and the early sunshine had
turned the tombs from drab grey-white to a mild yellow
ochre. Dew glistened on them, and the scent of earth and
grass and moisture swirled invigoratingly around me. A few
black birds rose from between the tombs and fluttered low
for a short distance before settling out of sight in another part
of the cemetery. I could hear them tweeting and lisping softly
amid the grass.

I began to search for the tomb that had been tampered
with. Several in this section, I noted, were large mausolean
structures. Big vaults like cottages. Each of them probably
held eight or a dozen coffins. On three of them I read inscrip-
tions involving the names of several persons. On one I read
dates going back to 1819, 1823, 1829 and 1833. It was this one
that seemed to me to have a suspicious look. It was of brick
and at least ten feet high, the façade being divided into eight
hollowed squares.

Looking closely, I was sure that the square at the upper right corner had been recently broached and then re-sealed. Whoever had removed the bricks and replaced them had done a very neat job, for at a distance of six feet or so no difference could be detected in relation to the other compartments. It was only because I had come here with the definite object of finding a tomb that had been tampered with that I noticed these minute traces of fresh cement in the spaces between the bricks. What seemed to confirm it was that at the base of the vault, in the grass, I saw one or two specks of cement dust.

The wind lisped in the grass, and I heard the black birds. In the south, somewhere far beyond the rugged cliff like a giant's shoulder under which I had stood the evening before, a dog was barking. Its earnest whoof-whoof somehow added to the peacefulness of the scene.

I decided to return to Eltonsbrody at once. I wanted to be in time to see Miss Linton off—if she had not left already.

Nearing the grounds, I heard the deep bark of a dog, and on going round the bend, I saw the slight figure of my hostess crossing a gully on my right. The two dogs on leash kept tugging her forward in their eagerness to advance. She reached the road just a few yards ahead of me, and waited for me to come up, smiling and greeting me: 'Mr. Holmes on the rampage so early?'

'Oh, I had a dip in the sea, then I went for a walk,' I said uncomfortably, though I tried hard to seem unconcerned.

'How far did you go? Anywhere near the cemetery?'

'Yes, just about there,' I said as we moved on along the road.

She made deprecatory sounds. 'You should have had your breakfast before going to look for that coffin, my boy. Since I was a girl I've heard it said that it's never healthy to go into a graveyard on an empty stomach.'

'Are you really concerned about my health, Mrs. Scaife, or could you possibly be afraid I'm getting warm in my search for the coffin?'

She smiled. 'My dear boy, fear is an emotion I haven't known during the past two or three days. Since getting out of bed on Wednesday morning I knew there would be no more need for me to fear anything from this life.'

I glanced at her but made no comment.

'That little incident I was alluding to the night before last when I came in to wish you a good night's rest—you remember?' She smiled, and I was struck by the kindly, even sad, light in her pale blue eyes. There was something very feminine in her at this moment—something fragile and weak. 'On Tuesday night, just after dinner, it happened. And on Wednesday morning I was certain. I knew then it was no accident in the strict sense of the word.'

'What are you talking about?' I asked. 'I haven't the faintest idea.'

'Oh, let's not bother to discuss it, my boy. Lovely morning, isn't it?' She took a deep breath. 'Air smells good. Enjoy it, Mr. Woodsley. Enjoy it. You're young. Don't enjoy it half-heartedly but with all the verve in you.'

As we were passing the car I remarked: 'I see somebody has left a car here. Have you any idea whom it could belong to?'

She chuckled. 'You're not a good actor, my boy.'

'Is Borkum spending the day at Eltonsbrody?'

She shrugged. 'Perhaps. Or perhaps in the cemetery. We never know what a sad, blighted soul like Borkum might not do. Poor fellow. Like myself, he has nothing to fear from life to-day—but he doesn't know it, and I won't tell him. It's better that he remains in ignorance.'

'Evidently you prefer me to remain in ignorance, too.'

'Oh, you're all right. You'll piece things together for yourself before long. And it won't be so long, either.'

As we were moving along the driveway I said: 'Perhaps you may be interested to know that because of your practical jokes Miss Linton is returning to Bridgetown. She's leaving by this morning's bus.'

'She is, is she? Oh, well, I daresay I can't blame her. I've made myself an awful nuisance, I'm sure. I take it another nurse will be coming in her place? Did she mention?'

'Yes. She phoned Doctor Dayton last night. I do hope this one will have the Mark so that she won't incur your dislike.'

'Let's hope so, my boy. Let's earnestly hope so. It's never a long chance, you know. As I've mentioned before, about three people in every ten have it.'

A little later, on going up to my room, I was dismayed to see that the time was long after seven. Miss Linton must be on her way already. The bus left at seven. Or was it seven-thirty? I hurried down to the kitchen to inquire, and Tappin told me that some mornings it was seven and some mornings seven-thirty.

'What's it this morning? Seven or seven-thirty?' I asked.

'Half-past seven, sir,' he said, 'but it won't pass here till about fifteen minutes after it leaves Martin's Bay.'

'Oh, you mean it leaves Martin's Bay at half-past seven?'

'Yes, sir. Mr. Woodsley, you going back to Bridgetown dis morning?'

'Me? No. But Nurse Linton is. She hasn't passed out yet, has she?'

'No, sir. Oi ain' see her pass out.'

'She must still be upstairs, then.'

Going upstairs again, I tapped on her door, but got no reply, so assumed she must be having a bath. I moved on to my room and got dressed in shorts and shirt, my usual attire since I had come to this part of the island. On my way downstairs I tapped again, but she had not yet come up, so I decided that the best thing would be to go down and wait in the sitting-room until she appeared.

The servants came into the dining-room for Prayers. Mrs. Scaife, in her olive-green dressing-gown, had just come down, Bible in hand.

I noticed that the glances they gave her were rather troubled, but she behaved as though unaware of anything unusual in their manner.

She smiled round in her old benevolent way.

After the Lessons, instead of proceeding to the Lord's Prayer as customary, she raised her hand and announced: 'Let us bow our heads in prayer.'

The servants seemed surprised, but not greatly so. They had the look as though prepared for anything odd this morning. They bowed their heads, and Mrs. Scaife cleared her throat and began to pray. For me, it was more a piece of poetry than a prayer. Perhaps that is why I remember it so clearly.

'Oh, gracious Father on high, to-day Thursday we find ourselves once again with the breath and pulse of this life which Thou in Thy great goodness and benevolence hast seen fit to bestow upon us. We thank Thee, oh Lord. We thank Thee for permitting us to open our eyes and focus our senses upon another of Thy kindly days. More than ever to-day we somehow feel deeply grateful to Thee for Thy sunshine and for Thy cooling winds and the greenness of Thy trees and the soft clouds against the blue of Thy infinite space. The sight of black birds flitting on the rocks and on the highway, the sight of the canefields and of the distant sea, oh Creator, comes upon us this day with a freshness and a yearning nostalgia that send our spirits back to the times of our humble youth. Keep alive in us this day the appreciation of these things. Teach us to value them to the last iota of their worth, for our time to tarry may not be long. Yea, the shadow of death may be dense upon our mortal forms, and the final trumpet blast may even at this moment be sounding. So let us breathe and live and revel in the unlimited sweetness of every second of every minute of every hour of this new day that is before us. Grant this to us, oh loving and kindly God. Grant this to us, we beseech Thee.'

On the last few words her voice fell to a murmur. She seemed to fall into a sad trance. There was a pause, then with a soft sigh she began: 'Our Father . . .' and the servants joined in the Lord's Prayer.

It was not until a minute or two later when they were dispersing that I suddenly realised that I had seen nothing of Miss Linton. Surely by now, I told myself, she should have passed upstairs on her way from the bathroom. The bathroom was on the ground-floor, as I think I have mentioned before.

I rose and entered the narrow passage-way that led to the bathroom and toilet. I stopped outside the door of the bathroom and listened. But there were no sounds of water or of anyone moving inside. I called: 'Miss Linton, are you in here?' But there was no answer. I tried the door and it opened. The room was empty, and the tiled floor was dry. No one had used the shower this morning.

I hurried upstairs and knocked on her door. There was no reply, so I went in. But there was no one in the room but the patient.

I glanced about and saw that Miss Linton's small suitcase, which had lain in the corner near the wash-stand, was missing —also the one or two garments she had had hanging behind the door on pegs. Her toilet things, too, had vanished from the dressing-table. This meant, I concluded, that she must have packed and left already. Rather odd, I thought. Surely she could have said hallo to me before rushing off. Not very flattering to my vanity.

After pottering about the room a bit, I went downstairs again. Went out to the kitchen and outside. Tappin was sharpening the blade of a cutlass at the foot of the steps.

I said: 'Tappin, are you sure you didn't see Nurse Linton go out?'

'No, sir. She ain' pass out. Oi woulda see her. Oi was round in de front garden since Oi come to work. It's only because of Prayers Oi come round dis way.'

'When did you come to work?'

'Since six o'clock, sir.'

'And from six until the time I spoke to you in the kitchen here before Prayers you say you were in the front garden?'

'Yes, sir. Oi was moulding up de roses in de tubs. Nobody pass out and go to de road whoile Oi was in de garden.'

I called Jackman. 'Jackman, have you seen anything of Miss Linton for the morning?'

'No, sir. Oi ain' see de young lady. She not upstairs wid Malverne?'

'No. She was supposed to be leaving for Bridgetown.'

'Sir, perhaps she gone to Martin's Bay to meet de bus.'

'But doesn't the bus pass the gate here? Why should she go all the way down to Martin's Bay to meet it?'

I noticed Tappin craning his head. Suddenly he exclaimed: 'Sir, Listen! De bus coming up de road yonder now. Ef you run out to de gate you will be in good toime to see ef de young lady in it.'

I dashed off at once.

A stoutish black woman with a basket was waiting by the side of the road. 'Waiting for the bus?' I asked her. And she smiled and said yes.

Almost at once we heard the laboured drone of the bus as it appeared up the steep incline. The woman stepped out into the middle of the road and held up her hand. The bus came to a stop and she got in.

I had ample time to examine the few passengers in it. Miss Linton was not there. Unbelieving, I stared after the bus as it continued on its way up the road. I stood there for a moment, glancing round at the iron gate of Eltonsbrody and at the casuarinas and mahoganies, and a cold numbness began to spread through my stomach.

20

I went into the house and looked for Mrs. Scaife. She was at breakfast, and as I entered she looked up and smiled at me. 'I was just wondering if you weren't going to have breakfast this morning, my boy.'

I gave her a cold stare and said: 'I've just been out to the road to have a look at the passengers in the bus.'

'Have you? Did you know of someone travelling to town?'

'Yes. Miss Linton. But she wasn't in the bus, Mrs. Scaife.'

'No? Oh, of course, you did mention she was going back to town—but shouldn't she have waited until her relief arrived?'

'Look, tell me. I want to know if you've seen anything of her since last night. A plain yes or no, please!'

She laughed with genuine amusement, giving me a teasing glance. 'No truly civilised person ever gives a plain yes or no to any question, and I pride myself on thinking I'm a civilised person.'

'Are you going to answer my question?'

She wiped her mouth with her napkin, still shaking with mirth. 'So much like Michael,' she murmured to her bacon. Then she glanced up with her affectionate twinkle and said: 'My boy, I really believe if you stayed in this house long enough I'd become so attached to you I'd have to hire Borkum to assist me in carving you up so that I could preserve your bones as a loving memento to a dear, dear young man.'

Without another word, I took my place and began to eat, for what with my sea bathe and the walk to the cemetery I was ravenously hungry.

She kept watching me quizzically throughout the meal, now and then uttering some flippant remark which I pretended not to hear.

I looked past her at the sideboard where the sunlight, as usual, was playing on the glassware and on the cloth draped over the edge. The clump of brain coral gazed back at me with its customary sly smile, sinister and inscrutable. The shadow of a green glass mug lay across it, giving it a new air of fantasy. Idly I wondered why the mornings before I hadn't noticed this green shadow, then it occurred to me that the mug had been moved. It used to stand far back on the sideboard. I noticed that within the green twilight that pervaded the interior there was a dark object—something long and slim, like a roll of paper, or a long envelope.

Mrs. Scaife followed my gaze and remarked: 'Is it the green mug you're interested in? It's a sealed envelope I've put into it. I put it in this morning when I came down. It's my last will and testament, as the solicitors say. I made it out yesterday, and took it down to Martin's Bay to get two of my old peasant acquaintances to sign as witnesses.'

She sighed, and her manner grew a trifle musing, a trifle sad. 'Of course, Mitchell will have to have this house, because it's entailed and must pass on to him. But my money is my own to dispose of as I please—and this furniture and my personal effects. I've willed these things to people I love.'

She glanced at me and smiled. 'My boy, I can see you're worried about your friend. I mean the nurse. Ah, well! I can't help it if I didn't like her, can I? It was just the same with Mitchell's wife. She hadn't the Mark, and I hated her just as much as I hated Mitchell himself. As a baby, he often came very near to death. I had to control myself not to strangle him. Ah, dear! But what a difference when Gregory came along! He had the Mark so strong on him that I found I could even tolerate Mitchell's presence in this house, so long as it meant having the little fellow with me, too. Try to understand me, Mr. Woodsley. Don't regard me as a lunatic. There are many strange people in this world, you know. Some are laughed at, and some are treated as mental cases—simply because the normal run of people don't understand their strangeness. Don't *attempt* to understand. I'm one of that kind. That's why I've never had any friends. Even my own parents despised me because of what they considered to be a streak of wanton cruelty in me. They couldn't see that I was *born* to revel in everything gruesome and deathly, that the sight of blood, instead of causing me abhorrence, gave me delight, sent me into breathless ecstasies. Why should I be condemned because I was born with a love of carnage? Why should I be considered mad because I can sense death on people? Why should I be denied the pleasure of indulging my deathly whims?'

She glanced out of the window. 'Ah! It's clouding over. I believe there's going to be rain. The sunset was very vivid yesterday. Mr. Woodsley, there are going to be tragic events to-day. I wish I could tell you what exact form they'll take, but my powers don't extend that far. I simply know that death hangs heavily over Eltonsbrody to-day. The shadow is dense—'

She broke off. A knock had sounded on the front door. I rose. 'I believe it's the doctor. I heard a car.'

I was right. It was Doctor Dayton, and with him was a tall-ish girl in nurse's uniform: 'Nurse Linton asked me to bring someone to relieve her,' he told us. 'This is Nurse Graham, Mrs. Scaife.'

'A pleasure to have her here,' smiled the old lady.

'Has Nurse Linton left already? She said something about taking the bus, but I asked her to wait until I came.'

Mrs. Scaife glanced at me. 'Mr. Woodsley can tell you. She's been confiding in him quite a lot. Has she left yet, my boy?'

'I have no idea whether she's left or not, doctor,' I said stiffly. 'She wasn't in the bus—that I know for certain. I went out to look.'

'Haven't you seen her for the morning?' he asked.

'I haven't. Her suit-case and things are not in the room upstairs, so she must have gone away.'

He seemed to sense that something was wrong, because he kept glancing from me to Mrs. Scaife in a puzzled manner.

Mrs. Scaife chuckled and said: 'I have an idea Mr. Woodsley suspects she's met with foul play, doctor.'

'What do you mean by that? Foul play?'

I flashed: 'Perhaps Mrs. Scaife knows why I think so!'

We had moved into the sitting-room now. The wind droned in at the open windows, bleak and with the promise of rain.

'Mr. Woodsley has been doing some splendid detective work in here, doctor. That's why I ventured to say he might know more than I do.' The old lady gave my arm a playful squeeze as she spoke. 'He's a dear young man, believe me. But he's suspicious of me. He thinks it very likely I've murdered Nurse Linton and carved her up.'

The doctor laughed—but in an embarrassed way. Nurse Graham smiled uncertainly. 'Anyway, shall we go up at once?' said the doctor.

I didn't accompany them upstairs. I lit a cigarette and stood at a window in the sitting-room looking at the sky which was one blanket of grey. A fine drizzle was falling. It came almost horizontal on the fresh wind. The hotels and cottages down at Bathsheba were hazed and indistinct, though towards Martin's Bay it was much clearer.

I heard footsteps. It was Mrs. Scaife. She had come downstairs. I saw her move towards the pantry.

The drizzle thickened. I shut the windows. I went into the dining-room. Footsteps sounded on the stairs, and the doctor came down.

'Could I have a word with you, Mr. Woodsley?'

'Certainly. Shall we go into the hallway?'

When we got there, he said: 'What's been happening here? Nurse Linton phoned me last night and said she couldn't remain on this case any longer. She gave me no details, and I'm a little puzzled.'

I told him about Mrs. Scaife's practical jokes.

'Why should she have done that? That's strange.'

'Have you been in attendance on her a long time, doctor?'

'Who? Mrs. Scaife? Yes. Since her husband died. I knew her husband very well. He was a personal friend.'

'What did he die from, by the way?'

'Cerebral haemorrhage.'

'There was nothing irregular about his death?'

'No. What makes you think there might have been?'

'I only wondered,' I said. Suddenly I told him briefly about what had been happening during the past few days. He was amazed, of course, and kept giving me frowning glances.

'I just can't—it seems fantastic,' he said. 'And this pail of blood—did you go back into that room this morning to see if—I mean, did you smell any blood in the corridor again?'

'No, I haven't been in there again—and I don't want to.'

'I'm worried about Miss Linton. What could have happened to her? I phoned both the hotels when I was upstairs and they've seen nothing of her.'

'The only thing I can assume,' I said, 'is that she must have gone down the road to meet the bus and some car gave her a lift to town.'

'When I get to town I'll ring you and let you know if she's got there safely. I must be off.'

I went in and was making for the pantry when the sound of voices caught my attention. It came from the stairs. Glancing up, I saw Mrs. Scaife in conversation with Nurse Graham.

Suddenly the old lady beckoned to me. 'Could you come up here, my boy?'

I joined them at the top of the stairs. Miss Graham was a plain-looking, rather timid creature. She had a hesitant smile.

'Mr. Woodsley,' said the old lady, 'Miss Graham has just made an important find.'

'What's that?'

'Tell him, Nurse.'

Miss Graham said: 'Well, I don't know if it's really important, but I thought I had to mention it. I was about to put my suit-case under the bed when I noticed that another one was there. It had the letters G.L. on it, so I thought it might be Miss Linton's. I called Mrs. Scaife, and we opened it and found her things in it—and—and there was a handkerchief, too, that—well, it just reeked of chloroform.'

21

I looked at Mrs. Scaife and said: 'There was no suit-case under the bed when I went into that room before breakfast.'

'Wasn't there, my boy? Are you sure?'

'Quite sure. I looked not only in the corner near the wash-stand where Miss Linton kept her suit-case but I searched everywhere. I distinctly remember lifting the bed-sheet and looking under the bed.'

'Tch, tch! Naturally. How silly of me not to have assumed that you would be thorough. Well, well. The mystery deepens.'

'Does it? May I see the suit-case and the handkerchief, Nurse?'

Mrs. Scaife followed us into the room. She stood behind me as I bent down and examined the contents of the suit-case. The handkerchief's strong chloroform fumes immediately struck me, and I straightened up. I took it up and looked at it, and saw the initials M S worked in faded blue thread at one corner. It was a man's handkerchief.

'Mrs. Scaife, I'd like to have a chat with you alone. Shall we go downstairs?'

'Certainly.'

Downstairs, I said: 'What have you done with her, Mrs. Scaife?'

She tittered. 'Why the sudden melodrama, my boy?'

'I want to know what you've done with her. Come on. Is she in that room upstairs? The doctor's old room?'

'And suppose she is, what of it? Do you want to rescue her?'

I stared at her a moment, then said: 'But why? Why did you have to do this? What have you put her in there for? Is that black brute in there with her, too?'

She made no reply. Only stared back at me, her expression unreadable.

The morning had darkened, and the wind and rain got more boisterous with the passage of every minute. Out of the corner of my eye I could see the epergne on the centre table, for we were in the sitting-room. It glimmered with a dirty, greenish unrealness. The air in the room felt laden with moisture, and the vagrant draughts were as active as always.

'Mrs. Scaife, I want an answer. Is Miss Linton in the doctor's old room upstairs?'

Suddenly she stiffened, and her gaze moved past me into the dining-room. I followed her gaze. 'What's the matter?' I asked.

Something seemed to hold her attention in the dining-room. Her face looked very pale, and her eyes gleamed with an unnatural light. She said: 'Mr. Woodsley, Malverne has just this instant died.'

Behind us, the windows shook dismally under the furious slamming assaults of the wind and rain. A leaf swirled in from the hallway, hesitated an instant, then wheeled its way lispingly across the floor, coming to a stop near the edge of the aged carpet. Perhaps two, even three, minutes might have elapsed, then footsteps sounded on the stairs, muffled by the swish and whine of the wind and rain. It was Nurse Graham. She came towards us and said: 'Mrs. Scaife, the girl—the patient is dead. She just died.'

'Very well, Nurse.'

The girl hesitated, glancing from the old lady to me.

'I'll have all arrangements made for the burial, Nurse.'

I said: 'Nurse, perhaps you'd better try and phone Doctor Dayton.'

Mrs. Scaife glanced at the nurse and said: 'It's all right. I'll speak to him later on.' She began to move towards the stairs, then paused and told the nurse: 'Just wait down here a moment, Nurse. I'll call you up as soon as I'm ready.'

'Very well, Mrs. Scaife.'

But I was determined not to be balked by this diversion. I strode after her and accompanied her upstairs. In the corridor she halted and smiled at me. 'Mr. Woodsley, you'd better go back downstairs and wait with the nurse.'

'I refuse,' I said. 'You're going to tell me where Miss Linton is. It's no use pretending any longer. I know she's fallen foul of you and your strangeness.'

'Tch, tch! So impetuous. Oh, dear! Yes, since you must know, we did chloroform her. That old handkerchief of my husband's should have clinched the matter in your mind, I'm sure.'

'Where is she? In the doctor's old room?'

'No. She's down at Martin's Bay in a fisherman's cottage. Strapped to a chair since half-past eleven last night and gagged to boot so that she can't make any noise. When she woke this morning—*if* she slept—there was a lovely sight for her to see. A coffin filled with bones from the cemetery. A grinning skull and ribs and femurs. Ha, ha! The biggest practical joke of all. And a lovely pail of blood, too. Go down and find her and relieve her of her misery, my boy. How I hate that creature! She was setting her cap at you, I'm certain!'

'Where is this cottage? What part of Martin's Bay is it situated?'

'Go and find it for yourself. Ask any of the fisher-people down there. No good my directing you from here. It won't help. Run along, you smitten boy! You can pop the question the minute you find her.'

I left her and hurried downstairs. At the kitchen door I nearly collided with Tappin.

'Mr. Woodsley, sir! What happening? Where you going?'

'Martin's Bay. Look here, I wonder if you can help me, Tappin. Do you know of any unoccupied cottages down there?'

'Unoccupied cottages? Yes, sir. They got one or two. But what wrong, sir? Anyt'ing happen?'

'Yes. And I've got to hurry. I have reason to believe that Miss Linton is down there, tied up and gagged, in one of the vacant cottages.'

'Tied up and gagged! Oi! How you mean, sir? How she can—?'

'Look, I can't stop to explain now.'

'Sir, you got to careful going down dere now. Landslides is happen sometimes when it rain heavy loike dis. Lemme come wid you and show you de way.'

'Can you? Good man. Come along.'

'De mistress moight quarrel, but ef you can explain to her—'

'Yes, that's all right. I'll deal with her, no fear.'

Piloted by Tappin, I stumbled my way through the wind and rain along steep, tortuous tracks, inquiring at every cottage we passed, just as a matter of routine. Down in the bay it did not take us long to find the two vacant cottages. They were both dilapidated cabin-like structures. The roofs were rotted and the shingled walls gaped with large jagged holes. They were quite past the stage where anyone could live in them.

In neither of them could we find any trace of Miss Linton.

We persisted, asking at every cottage, but no one had seen any strange young lady, and there were no other unoccupied cottages for us to search in. By one o'clock Tappin and I were both weary from our tramping round. We were drenched.

Then one shortish old fellow told us: 'De only person who been down here was de ole lady from Eltonsbrody, sir. Ole Mrs. Scaife. She come down here yesterday and ask me cousin and his sister to soign a paper for her.'

'Yes, her will. She mentioned that to me this morning,' I said.

Working back towards the western end of the bay, we met a farmer called Hart whom Tappin knew well. From him we got a piece of information that alarmed me. He said that his son, a fisherman, had hired a boat to Mrs. Scaife. He pointed to a rock on the beach. 'Look at it dere, sir. Dat lil' skiff. She say she won't need it till dis evening.'

'Did she say what she needed it for?'

'No, sir. She didn't say. But she pay Tom handsome for it, sir.'

The rain hissed spitefully at us. The wind and the huge foaming waves on the beach created a turbulent rumble of sound that was almost palpable. The air reeked of fish and seaweed. I glanced towards the rock where the skiff was safely moored. It was well out of reach of the waves. I felt a sort of irresolution, and was about to suggest returning to Eltonsbrody when Hart said: 'Sir, you look fatigue. Why you don't come in and lemme give you somet'ing to eat before you cloimb up back to de house?'

'Well, that's very nice of you, Hart,' I said. 'And I'm going to take you at your word, because I'm ravenous.'

The meal, which consisted of fried flying fish, boiled sweet potatoes and pigeon peas and a large mug of cocoa, went a long way towards raising my spirits. We sat in the tiny sitting-room of Hart's cottage, each with a plate in his lap, for there was no room at the small table to accommodate even three people, and the table was already crowded with glassware and crockery of a diverse type (I don't remember seeing two cups or glasses that were exactly alike). Hart was a widower, though the wife of a neighbour cooked for him.

The meal over, I thanked Hart for his kindness, but he laughed and said: 'No, sir. Don't t'ank me. T'ank Mary who cook for me. She always cook big so plenty leff over. Dat's why Oi risk to offer you somet'ing.'

'Anyway, before I go back to Bridgetown, I'm going to come down and look you all up,' I said. 'Now let's hurry back up to the house, Tappin. I have a nasty feeling I should be up there to keep an eye on things. Miss Graham may be needing me to boost her morale. Come on.'

The wind and rain chattered and whisked at our backs as we made our way up the winding difficult track. More than once boulders would come rattling down—not large ones, but they served to remind me of what Tappin had said about landslides. In some places the track was a rushing, gurgling torrent; reddish-amber water swirling around our ankles.

At length, the grey bulk of Eltonsbrody appeared ahead of us beyond a hump of land bristling with sisal grass. The last hundred yards seemed to stretch out into a mile, but, at last, we plodded our way through the back gate into the back-yard.

The first person we saw was McTurk hurrying towards the goat-pens, his head and shoulders covered with flour-bags. I hailed him and he halted and stared at us. 'Mr. Woodsley, sir! You come back?'

'What's been happening, McTurk? Is your mistress still in the house? She hasn't been out, has she?'

'No, sir. Miss Dahlia upstairs. She didn't go nowhere. In dis wedder, sir? How she could go out?'

'Miss Dahlia didn' ask for me, McTurk?' Tappin asked anxiously.

'No, she ain' ask,' growled McTurk, frowning, 'but you know full well de mistress never loike you to go out widdout telling her first.'

'I asked him to come with me,' I said. I glanced towards the kitchen door. I saw Jackman beckoning to me. She was calling, her voice muffled by the savage weather.

'What's it, Jackman?' I called back.

'Sir, de young lady in de dining-room asking for you. We was wondering where you gone to!'

I approached her and asked: 'What young lady? Miss Linton?'

'No, sir. De new nurse.' Then she exclaimed: 'Oh, lawd! Look how you soaking wet, sir! Lemme get you somet'ing to drink.'

'Thank you, Jackman. I'll go to the dining-room and see Miss Graham.'

Miss Graham rose from a chair at the dining-table. Her face looked puzzled and worried—even a little frightened. 'Mr. Woodsley, I couldn't imagine what had happened to you. My goodness, you're in a state!'

'What are you doing down here, Nurse?'

'That's what I wanted to speak to you about. I haven't been able to get into the room upstairs since I came down here this morning.'

'Why? Did Mrs. Scaife—?'

'Mrs. Scaife has locked herself in the room. I've knocked and called out to her until I'm tired, but I can't get an answer.'

'You mean since you came down here to tell us that the patient was dead you haven't been able to get into the room?'

'Yes, since then I've been down here. Over four hours. I just can't understand it. Mrs. Scaife won't open the door. And my suit-case is in there with all my things.'

'Did you hear any movement in the room?'

'Yes, she was doing something. I—I heard a sound as

though she was using tools—or instruments or something. The keyhole is blocked up.'

Jackman appeared with a tall tumbler of yellow liquid. 'Look, sir. Drink dis. It's a egg-flip Oi make for you. A lil' rum in it, sir. It will keep out de chill from you' bones.'

'By George, you're a brick, Jackman! Just the thing I need!' I took a sip and asked: 'Where's Bayley, by the way?'

'He gone to Horse Hill to get hibiscus bush for de goats, sir. Oi hear McTurk sending him off lil' whoile ago. You want anyt'ing?'

'Yes. Ask McTurk to go out on the road and see if an old car is parked under the big sandbox tree. Tell him to hurry. It's important.'

'Oi will tell him now, sir.' She hurried out.

'Nurse, you remain downstairs here,' I said to Miss Graham. 'I'll go up alone to see what's happening to the old lady.'

I finished the egg-flip and went upstairs. Draughts, as though gone mad like everything else in the house, danced and whirled about me so that I imagined I could see them describing rings and spirals round my head. There was a continuous whistle and whine in the windward rooms, and the wardrobe creaked at regular two-second intervals. The whole house seemed to sway and quiver in the strong wind-gusts.

At my knock on the door, I heard a slight movement within. 'Open this door at once, Mrs. Scaife! Come on! Open it!'

I heard a gasp—then nothing more for such a long interval that I knocked again and shouted: 'Did you hear me? Open the door! If you don't open it I'll smash it down! And I mean that!'

'Did you find Miss Linton?'

'No! I didn't—because she's probably still in this house. And you have got to tell me all about it and let me into the other rooms, too! Hurry up. I'm in a nasty mood!'

I heard a chuckle—then suddenly came a click in the lock, and the door opened.

'Since you insist, very well, my boy. Come in and have a look!'

I stared past her. Stared past her and saw something I shall not forget if I live to ninety.

22

She was smiling sweetly, benevolently—the same dear old lady. The mild, twinklingly humorous Mrs. Scaife who had greeted me so hospitably on the evening of Maundy Thursday. The same gentle mocker who had taken a pleasure in baiting me during the past few days. She waved her hand and said in a voice soft and sighingly contented: 'There you are, my boy! Tell me what you think. Isn't that a really pretty sight!'

The pretty sight was what the corpse of Malverne had been converted into. The marble-topped washstand had been cleared of the toilet receptacles. Now it was piled with human remains—two legs cut up neatly and expertly into sections and arranged in an orderly clump at one end of the washstand. At the other end, as though for symmetrical effect, sections of arms stood in another clump. In the middle lay the torso disembowelled and with the shaven head of the girl set in the middle of the glistening coiled mass of intestines. The mouth gaped rigidly, the eyes stared blue and glassy.

On the floor near the washstand lay a white enamel surgical tray containing water under whose surface gleamed several surgical instruments. The water was a pinkish brown. A smell of blood and flesh hung in the air, and my gaze travelled round and rested on a white enamel pail that stood in the corner near the wardrobe. It was half-filled with thick clots of blood.

I could say nothing. A numbness seemed to spread slowly through my stomach. Vaguely a panicked impulse to turn and rush downstairs came alive in me, but somehow I couldn't move.

'I enjoyed myself, my boy,' said the old lady. 'Oh, it was lovely, lovely! And you annoying young man! You wanted to deprive me of my fun! That's why I had to send you off to

Martin's Bay on a wild goose chase. It was your own fault. Tolerance is what matters, Mr. Woodsley. If only we could learn to smile and wink at each other's vices! Prudery is the most disgusting plague of mankind. But there, there! I mustn't moralise at this time of day—and in this weather. It's indecent. I have so many other interesting things to show you.'

She moved across the room to the door of the small room. She inserted a key into the lock, turned it and then pushed the door open. 'Come,' she called. 'Come and see. Have a look, my boy!'

Automatically I crossed and stopped beside her and looked into the room.

On the small bed lay the skeleton of a child—a child of about six or seven, to judge by its length. The bones seemed linked together with bits of thread, and it was dressed in a boy's tweed shorts and shirt, and a small cricket cap rested at an angle on the skull. A faint sickly-sweet smell came to my nostrils.

'My dear, dear little grandson Gregory who died on Monday. See what love can drive a doting old lady to do, my boy! This is what I paid a thousand dollars for. Borkum is such a versatile fellow, and such an expert anatomist!' She tittered. 'And so good at robbing graves! But I shouldn't slander the poor man. Robbing graves isn't a habit of his. It was done at my request. A special job. Like the one years ago—on the thirteenth of January, 1950.'

She smiled and sighed softly. 'Yes, my boy. In the room over there the doctor's skeleton reclines on the bed. I have him decked off in evening clothes—we Barbadians insist on correct dress, even for the dead. The clothes have got a bit moth-eaten now, of course, but never mind! It's been nice to know that I had such a vital part of my dear Michael with me in this house. His fleshly remains are in there, too. In a neat leaden box built over with a mound of earth like a miniature tomb. Gregory's remains have been treated in the same way—the fleshly remains. Heart, liver, entrails, and all the tissue scraped off the bones. But there was no space in this room here, so I had to have them left in the doctor's room. I'm sure you must have smelt fresh earth in the corridor two or three nights ago—the night you heard the bump. Remember? Borkum, clumsy fool that he is, dropped the leaden box. Good thing it was well sealed. I was furious with him. Suppose the box had burst and spilled its contents over the floor! I so hate a mess!'

She waved her hands towards the washstand. 'You can see for yourself what a neat, tidy job I've made of Malverne. Good gracious! What's that?'

Above the weather noise there came a deep rumble. It was not thunder, I was certain. It was too leisurely a sound, and it ended suddenly in a dull sort of bump.

Mrs. Scaife looked at me. 'Do you know what that is, Mr. Woodsley? It's a landslide.'

The house seemed to rock gently with a new vibration—a troublousness that seemed to seep up out of the earth. Mrs. Scaife wagged her head. 'I wonder if any lives have been lost. If the weather hadn't been so fierce I'd have taken a walk to see. Dead bodies fascinate me so much! Death, death! The one luscious adventure we can every one of us look forward to without any fear of disappointment. Isn't it satisfying to contemplate on, my boy?'

She must have continued in this vein for fully five minutes longer, and I simply had to stand there and listen to her.

'. . . I'd have taken you into the doctor's room to show you the skeleton in there, but Borkum is at work now. He's packing the bones and the leaden boxes into my old travelling trunk. He'll come in here for Malverne's remains, too, and little Gregory's skeleton. I want everything dumped into the sea. I've got a boat down there in the bay, and towards evening Borkum would have gone down with the trunk and put it into the boat and rowed out near the Well Pit. Borkum is a good boatman. He could manage safely. But I'm afraid the weather has upset our plans, so he's got to venture down earlier—perhaps in an hour's time. None of my keepsakes must remain in this house for unsympathetic eyes and hands to violate. Everything must be disposed of because my time is short. The Shadow is dense on me, my boy. On Tuesday evening I watched it flit by my window, but I'd put it down to an accident—just one of those little psychic accidents that happen to us strange people occasionally. But on Wednesday morning when I got up I knew it had been no accident. The gloom had settled on my shoulder, and I knew that for me it was only a matter of a few days. I have no idea how it will come to me, but death is near, Mr. Woodsley. For Borkum, too, though I haven't told him. I saw the Shadow on him since Monday evening when he brought little Gregory's body.'

She gave another of her sighs and said: 'Yes, on your friend, too. Miss Linton. I saw it on her when she arrived on Tuesday evening. The Shadow. And something told me that she was meant for me. For my pleasure. For my supreme ecstasy. And as my time was short, I said to myself why shouldn't I have a revel of gruesome fun before the end? Nothing to fear from the law, so why not? They can't hang me. Long before they discover that she's missing and attempt to arrest me I'll be dead. You see now why I've been so careless in dropping clues for you to find, my dear Holmes? You see now why I've been so free in talking about my doings and plans?'

'Mrs. Scaife! What are you trying to tell me? Where is Miss Linton? Have you done anything to her?'

She chuckled. 'I believe you are in love with her. Just step into the room there and lift the bedsheet. Look under dear little Gregory's bed and sigh a deep, long sigh, my boy.'

I hurried into the small room, bent and lifted the bed-sheet.

There was nothing under the bed.

I turned but the door had closed. I heard the key click in the lock. I knocked and shouted. 'Open the door, you bloody fiend! Open it!'

But there was no reply.

I looked through the keyhole and saw her cross the room and take the sheet from the bed. She spread it over the gruesome array of Malverne's remains on the wash-stand. Then she moved out of view.

I went to the window and discovered that it had been nailed to the sill. The nails were new ones.

Suddenly, above the noise outside I heard voices in the larger room. I began to hammer on the door again with my fists. I looked through the keyhole but only a corner of the bed and the washstand appeared in my range of vision. I recognised Jackman's voice. Then I heard Mrs. Scaife shout: 'What is the meaning of this, Jackman! Don't you know it is forbidden for you to come upstairs here!'

'Mistress, Oi had to come,' I heard Jackman say, and her voice sounded hysterical. 'Bayley jest come back from Horse Hill, mistress. 'E say a big landslide happen near de cemetery and de house me sister and cousin living in get buried. Mistress, you can let me run off to see what happen to dem? Me sister got two young children . . .'

At this point her mistress interrupted her. 'Did I hear you say there was a landslide near the cemetery?'

'Yes, Miss Dahlia. Oi hear de land fall down 'pon part of de graves and bury dem—'

'What! What's that! The graves! Oh, my God! What of the doctor's tomb, Jackman? Has anything happened to it? Has it been damaged?'

'Mistress, Oi ain' know. Bayley ain' say nutting—'

'Oh, my God! Quick! Get out of my way! I must go and see for myself. Oh, my God! Michael's tomb!'

I heard the footsteps receding into the corridor. I began to hammer on the door again, but Jackman, too, must have hurried out after her, for no one came to open the door.

I crossed to the window again, and looked through its streaming panes at the scene outside. I could make out the poultry-runs and the goat-pens, the back fence and the gate, but beyond that all I could see was a greyish-white pall of misty rain-drops. Here and there a maypole stalk from a clump of sisal grass reared itself dimly like some ghostly skeleton.

Eltonsbrody might have been a house drifting among the clouds. The very foundations seemed to creak under the strain of the driving wind and the fierce slashing drops; I could well imagine what it would be like if a hurricane had come along instead of this savage rainstorm.

Suddenly I heard footsteps in the next room. I ran across to the door and started my hammering tattoo again, and called out: 'Who's in there! Open the door!'

There were quick footsteps in the next room, then the key clicked in the lock and the door opened. It was Miss Graham.

'Mr. Woodsley! What are you doing in here? Did she lock you in?'

'She did. Has she gone out? I've got to get after her.'

'But where's the corpse? What's happened to it?'

'The washstand,' I said briefly. 'She's out of her mind. Look, better get back downstairs—and stay downstairs. Do you hear me? Keep in the kitchen with the servants.' I hurried out of the room and she accompanied me downstairs. We found Tappin and Bayley in the dining-room.

'Sir, you hear about de landsloide?' Bayley began excitedly, but I cut him short. 'Where is your mistress? She went out, didn't she?'

'Yes, sir,' Tappin said. 'She gone running out in de rain. She gone to see ef de doctor' tomb get damaged. Sir, remember Oi tell you about Miss Dahlia and dat tomb! She will kill herself ef anyt'ing happen to dat tomb. She worship it.'

McTurk entered and said: 'Mr. Woodsley, de car still dere outsoide by de roadsoide near de sandbox tree.'

'Oh, good. Thanks, McTurk. Well, look here, Tappin, you and McTurk remain in the house here with Miss Graham. Understand? Don't leave her under any circumstances. And keep an eye on the stairs. Don't go upstairs, but keep an eye on the stairs. I believe there's somebody in the doctor's room.'

'Who dat, sir?'

I hesitated, then told him: 'Borkum—the fellow who

worked here in the doctor's time. I'm off. Can't wait to explain anything more.'

The wind and rain struck me like a vast cold living quilt. I had to brace myself to advance against it. I took the track that led round the house to the driveway.

I cut across country, but almost regretted it, for the gullies were raging pools across which I had to battle my way. A network of little rivers fed these pools, and in one place I nearly sank to my waist. I climbed up over a hump of land and saw the road glistening in the rain. I broke into a trot, and as I went round a bend I saw people ahead of me. The landslide must have attracted them. Drenched like myself, they plodded their way through the slashing drops. The road was slippery and treacherous and more than once I barely saved myself from coming a cropper, especially as I was now going downhill.

Rounding another bend, I saw a crowd standing about in a gully to my right—that is, to the east of the road. I paused, wondering whether I had missed my way, for the scene was confused. A huge mass of boulders and earth lay piled up on the eastern side of the depression, and the roof of a small cottage protruded greyly—a corrugated iron roof that glistened in the welter of pelting moisture. One or two men were digging with shovels, and I could hear the sobs and whimpering of women.

Suddenly I realised that the cemetery was just ahead—beyond the next bend in the road. I hurried on, and had no sooner got round the bend—it was the sharp, awkward bend—when I saw Mrs. Scaife. She was scrambling down the incline into the depression where the cemetery was situated. At a glance I could see what had happened. The eastern and part of the southern portion of the cemetery had been buried under a fall of land. The giant shoulder that had jutted so ominously above me the evening before when I had stood under the cliff and heard the tapping sounds made by Borkum had collapsed. The western section of the cemetery seemed unaffected, though small clumps of earth and a few boulders lay scattered in the grass between the tombs.

I went sliding and stumbling down the incline after the old lady. She had already reached the doctor's tomb when I caught up with her. She was blowing hard, her hair limp and wet, straggling down about her neck and shoulders. I caught her by a shoulder and spun her round. I uttered a few obscenities adding: 'And now come on! *This* time you aren't going to get out of it. What have you done with the remains of Miss Linton? I suppose you've cut her up as you did Malverne?'

She laughed a whimpering kind of laugh and gasped: 'You've guessed, have you? Yes, I cut her up. Borkum and I. Oh, it was such fun! '

'You beast! You beast!' I slapped her face hard, and she staggered off a few paces. She collided with her husband's tomb which was quite intact, and then she raised her face and looked past me. Her eyes widened. She cowered back, and I turned my head to follow her gaze.

There was a humming and a clattering crunch of earth, a shriek, harsh and metallic. I leapt away wildly, landed face down in the wet grass, felt mud and water and the salty taste of blood in my mouth, heard a crashing, yelling pandemonium almost on top of me. A hot pain knifed through my left arm, and then there was a clatter and swish, and long black lines seemed to darken the sky as I rolled over and glanced up. I shrank back, rolled over again in a panic, burying my face in the grass, felt myself flattened down under an abrupt weight, felt the breath being knocked out of me. A dull pain moved in my chest and spiralled round to my back and down to my legs.

I lay quiescent for a moment, hearing confused voices above me. I tried to rise, and found myself emerging from a pile of sugar-canes. People were running along the road above. Two men were scrambling down the incline. Not six feet from where I stood lay an overturned lorry hissing in the rain, a brownish wisp of vapour rising from among the differentials and the confused mass of sugar-canes that seemed to surround me on every side. I felt weak and dazed. The rain beat down on me with unabated spitefulness. I tried to stagger away towards the incline. A mist began to shift before my gaze, first red, then brown—then black. Through this blackness I was conscious of myself collapsing amid a shifty mass of rubble which I seemed to realise dimly had once been the doctor's tomb.

23

Later, I discovered that it was Jackman who had identified me. She had been among the crowd digging around the buried cottage. Fortunately none of my bones were broken. It was late afternoon when I came to on the bed in my room at Eltonsbrody, and Nurse Graham and Doctor Dayton were the first persons I became aware of. They were standing near the window in conversation. It was from them that I learnt that Mrs. Scaife was dead. The lorry-driver, too, had been killed, and another man who had been in the vehicle suffered serious injuries.

The doctor wanted to take me back to Bridgetown that evening, but, somehow, I felt that it would have been letting down the servants to clear out like that and leave everything in confusion. I had grown very attached to them within the few days of my stay in the house. And, apart from this, I wanted to satisfy my curiosity concerning several little matters.

I didn't regret this decision. After the doctor and the nurse had left (the doctor promised to make arrangements with the undertakers concerning Mrs. Scaife's corpse and to inform her son, Mitchell, and, of course, the police) Tappin and I made a careful tour of the house.

In the doctor's room we discovered traces of earth on the floor near the bed, but there were no bones on the bed as I had anticipated. To our great surprise, we found that the wardrobe had crashed forward and lay at an acute angle over what seemed to be a trunk. Stooping, I played about the beam of my torch to see whether it would be possible to edge out the trunk from under the huge monster of mahogany.

A black warted face, tongue protruding, eyes bulging rigidly, met my gaze.

It was not until the following day that we attempted to have the wardrobe shifted. It must have crashed down upon Borkum as he had been bending over the open trunk (the old-fashioned travelling trunk from the adjoining room). Two front leg-rests, one in the centre and a corner one, were rotten and in a crumbled state. No doubt all the unusual activity in the room after such a long period during which no one had entered it, must have caused a slight shift in the position of the wardrobe, and one of the circling draughts shot into the room during the rainstorm must have tipped it over too far in its perpetual swaying. Borkum had been pinned down, his neck caught between the front of the wardrobe and the edge of the trunk. In the trunk we discovered the doctor's bones, the ribs and legs and arms clothed in a moth-eaten, dusty evening suit, stiff-fronted shirt blotched and yellow, and black bow-tie.

On the washstand in the next room we found a sealed envelope with the name *Tappin* written on it in beautiful copperplate. Inside it there was a sheet of paper on which there was more beautiful copperplate. I made a copy of it so can quote it word for word here:

> *Tappin—I can't leave this house to you servants because the law won't let me. It's entailed and must go to Mr. Mitchell. But all I have, my money in the bank and my other possessions, I leave to you four servants. This is only a little friendly note to you, Tappin. My will properly drawn up is downstairs in the green mug on the sideboard. In it I have allotted to each of you what you must have, and I'm sure I have tried to be as fair as anyone can be. One favour I must ask you, Tappin. Please take care of my husband's tomb. Have it painted over every six months as is my custom, and see that no weeds are allowed to grow around it. But please never*

have it broken open for any reason whatsoever. That tomb must never be defiled. I want it to remain intact and as a monument to a Man—a man who loved me and was kind to me, who was tolerant of my strangeness in whatever seemingly terrible and disgusting form it took. So please take good care of that tomb for me. And, Tappin, try like my dear husband not to think too ill of your old Miss Dahlia whatever happens and whatever you may hear of her that is ugly. Some of us poor mortals, you know, were meant from birth to go through this life 'leaning all awry'.

Well, there you have it all. Not a pretty tale. And as for the central figure in it, I can only leave it to you to decide what sort of person she was. Up to this moment I haven't yet made up my mind about her. I somehow simply can't bring myself to dismiss her out of hand as a homicidal maniac. If you'd been in my place and been able to hear her chuckle, and watch her mild, benevolent face break into a twinkling, mischievous smile you'd more readily understand what I mean. Could it really be that she had been born with some macabre trait peculiar only to her? It sounds absurd, I know, yet . . . Anyway, what I know is that many times when I think back on her I find a sort of sadness moving inside me. Perhaps she was right. Perhaps there's something dark in me myself that makes me able to feel sympathy for her in spite of her horrible deeds. The only times when my sympathy gives way to a cold, bitter fury are those moments when I picture myself standing in the north-eastern section of the little cemetery watching the rough wooden coffin with Nurse Linton's chopped up remains being taken out from the old family vault. In these moments I feel nothing but hate and loathing for the old lady.

Sometimes I forget her entirely and only the house stands out in my memory. There are quite a few nights when I wake up and hear a ghostly drone of wind outside, persistent, monotonous, whooping and whining—and the creaking of a wardrobe. Even as I sit here writing this I can swear that into the corner of my eye the pale green spectre of an epergne is sidling, elegant and elusive, nodding at me in a sort of dim mockery. And a draught is tickling its way up my trousers legs. A sideboard is taking shape, and that sinister-looking lump of brain coral is forcing me to turn my head to look at it. It's going to be a long time before I succeed in shaking off the atmosphere of that place. The very name Eltonsbrody seems like a ragged, sticky piece of cobweb that will cling for all time round the nerve-cells of my brain.